All rights reserved. No part of this book may be reproduced in any form by any electronic or mechanical means including photocopying, recording, or information storage and retrieval without permission in writing from the author.

The Third Call
Paperback Copyright © 2020 Lorhainne Ekelund
Editor: Talia Leduc

All rights reserved.
ISBN-13: 978-1989698341

Give feedback on the book at:
lorhainneeckhart@hotmail.com

Twitter: @LEckhart
Facebook: AuthorLorhainneEckhart

Printed in the U.S.A

THE THIRD CALL

The O'Connells

LORHAINNE ECKHART

"A new family series more suspenseful than the Friessens."

Karen L. Vine Voice

"Deputy Marcus O'Connell has a sixth sense when it comes to crime, honed by a troubled childhood. So when a young girl calls, asking for help, he finds himself in a hostage situation of sorts with a disillusioned ex-military and a homeless single mother."

Honest Bookworm

"This book masterfully interweaves several hot button topics and evokes feelings of anger, sympathy and even shock. A scared little girl and her calls for help are the catalyst to a situation that quickly spirals out of control and ends in tragedy."

(Rebmay)

About the O'Connells

The O'Connells of Livingston, Montana, are not your typical family. Follow them on their journey to the dark and dangerous side of love in a series of romantic thrillers you won't want to miss. Raised by a single mother after their father's mysterious disappearance eighteen years ago, the six grown siblings live in a small town with all kinds of hidden secrets, lies, and deception. Much like the contemporary family romance series focusing on the Friessens, this romantic suspense series follows the lives of the O'Connell family as each of the siblings searches for love.

The O'Connells

The Neighbor
The Third Call
The Secret Husband
The Quiet Day
The Commitment, An O'Connell Novella
The Missing Father
The Hometown Hero
Justice
The Family Secret
The Fallen O'Connell
The Return of the O'Connells
And The She Was Gone
The Stalker
The O'Connell Family Christmas

The Third Call

Deputy Marcus O'Connell is blindsided one night after a series of calls comes in from an unknown number, and the caller on the other end is a child. All he knows is she's six years old, her name is Eva, and there's someone in her house who wants to hurt her.

Marcus is the ultimate bad boy turned deputy. He knows everything about how to get away with something, considering he was one of the middle of the six O'Connell siblings. He never had responsibility resting on his shoulders like his brother Owen, and he's never been the center of attention like his little sister, Suzanne. Marcus knows how to find trouble and talk his way out of it.

Now, as the head deputy for the Livingston sheriff's office, he knows everything about everybody, and no one can pull anything over on him. It's why he's such a damn good deputy. But even Marcus dreads what cops know as the third call.

When Marcus takes the call the first time, he thinks it's a prank. The second time, he knows there's a problem. The third time the call comes in and is patched through to him, he knows it's something he can't ignore. The only thing is, the girl is terrified and keeps hanging up, and Marcus knows someone is in the house with her.

Where are her parents, and who is this mysterious girl who needs his help?

Chapter One

Deputy Marcus O'Connell took another swallow of Suzanne's favorite local stout and wondered how his sister could drink the stuff. He'd never taken to heavy dark beer, preferring lighter lagers, and he was drinking it now only because she'd ordered two and slid one over to him just after he got there. Now, she was making her way over to one of the firefighters, Lieutenant Toby Chandler.

"Stop staring at them," said Sheriff Osbert Berry, Bert for short, who was sitting on the same stool at the end of the bar where he always sat, nursing the ale on tap. Marcus hadn't known he was paying attention.

"I'm not staring. I'm observing. There's a difference." He leaned on the bar, having to glance back over his shoulder to Bert, who seemed to have packed on a few more pounds as of late. He already had a hefty frame for a man in his sixties, and it appeared he hadn't shaved in days.

"Bullshit, Marcus," Bert said. "You're staring them down with that look you have that makes everyone nervous. She's flirting, blowing off steam. Let her have some fun, and remember, son, you're talking to the man who wrote the book on staring down numbskulls whose asses you want to kick. I trained you. I know you better than anyone."

For a second, Bert smiled almost fondly over at Suzanne, who he still couldn't believe was making eyes at Toby. Why couldn't she see that his only redeeming quality was the fact that he showed up for work? His sister was one of the best firefighters in Livingston, and if push came to shove, it would be her Marcus wanted saving his ass, not the asshole she was making eyes at.

"I mean, look at him," Marcus said, "the way he looks down at her with that flashy plastic smile he puts on for every girl. Why the hell can't she see the guy's a player, shallow, got nothing going for him? Lost count of the number of times I've told her to look anywhere else. She's been with the department longer, yet he got the promotion to lieutenant last week. Give you three guesses as to why he got it and not her."

He dragged his gaze back down the bar as his sister tossed her hair over her shoulder and shrugged, flirting. He had to look away. The sheriff was softly chuckling under his breath, then polished off the pint in front of him and gestured to Ken, the bartender and owner of the Lighthouse bar, a silver-haired former golden-gloves fighter and someone else he had to keep an eye on.

"What, you mean just because he's a strapping young white man who has the same last name as the former chief?" Bert said as Ken slid him another pint. He nodded in thanks, then lifted his gaze to Marcus, who was counting the number of pints he'd downed—five or six, he thought. "Take a look in the mirror, son. Some could say the same about you." Bert's blue eyes were bloodshot with the sorrow that seemed to be a part of him now, so many months since he'd put his wife in the ground.

"Seriously, what the hell does that have to do with anything?" Marcus said. "I'm fucking good at what I do, and I didn't step over anyone or have anything handed to me. Doors weren't all that open for me, if you recall."

In fact, he was one of the six O'Connell kids, the brood who had been known as walking trouble—the kind of reputation their mom had warned them would be forever burned in the townsfolk's minds. He had frequently found himself in trouble as a kid, so much so that Bert had taken to picking him up immediately whenever someone did something, just to save time tracking him down. Constantly being one step from juvie had made him pick up on the kinds of things everyone else missed. Whether at accidents or crime scenes, he now had a sixth sense, just knowing who had done what before anyone could even make notes or grab a coffee. Maybe he just knew exactly how someone living a life of crime would think. If he didn't know the who, he just about always knew the why and the how.

The sheriff lifted his hand to stop him. "Just making a point is all, Marcus. You think I don't know all that? Well, what I know doesn't matter. People forget all that when shit hits the fan. We're not all balanced and politically correct and everything—and that kind of thing now matters, as was pointed out to me this morning by the city council." Bert gave him a significant glance.

Marcus gave everything to the old man he'd once looked up to. "What exactly was pointed out and by who?" he said, then looked down at the dark stout. He just couldn't make himself drink it, so he pushed it away. What had his sister been thinking, ordering it for him? Oh, yeah, she'd been distracted over Toby at the other end of the bar. Just then, Toby lifted his chin to Marcus as if they were friends, so he dragged his gaze back over to the sheriff, who leaned on the bar and lifted his pint of ale to take another swallow.

"Oh, you know," Bert said, "the same old crew, the mayor and all his cronies. Apparently, they want to see us more diverse and colorful. We've been told to hire a woman for the open deputy position."

For a second, he wasn't sure he'd heard correctly. "What open deputy position?"

Bert made a face. "The one the city council advised me of. Apparently, the backlog of paperwork and reports, budgets and stuff—ones I supposedly finished, signed, and submitted—showed that for the first time, the sheriff's office is actually in the black when it comes to closing cases. In fact, we're listed among the top fifty offices with the lowest numbers of unsolved crimes, or something along those lines, for whoever comes up with that kind of stuff. Funny thing is, though, I couldn't remember submitting all that paperwork."

Marcus wasn't sure what to say. The sheriff seemed to consider something as he looked around the bar. "Look, Sheriff…" he started before the old man rested his beer on the bar and cut him off.

"I know you've been covering for me," he said. "I know you're the one who's made sure everyone is getting where they need to be, getting the office staffed, giving tickets to keep the revenue coming in, making sure cases are being closed and lines aren't being crossed so this place stays safe. You make sure all the Ts are crossed and no one fucks up anywhere. I knew it was you, always did. In case I haven't said it, thank you. My head hasn't been in it, you know…" He stopped talking, and that sadness returned. So did the knot in Marcus's stomach as he thought of the day the call had come in. Peach Berry had

had a heart attack at the hair salon while getting her roots done. The dye had still been in her hair. His sister had been first on the scene, and he'd been second. He didn't think he'd ever forget the way the old man had cried.

"Stop it," Marcus said. "It's what we do. So we get extra help now? Good. I guess as long as it's someone who can do the job and is qualified…"

Case in point in terms of a lack of qualifications, in his mind, was Toby Chandler at the end of the bar, who was not only flirting openly with his sister but also taking in every hot woman in the room.

His cell phone buzzed, and he pulled it out, seeing the sheriff's office on the screen. "O'Connell," he said. The sheriff was now giving him everything.

"Sorry to bug you, Marcus," said Charlotte Roy, their dispatcher. "I know you're off, but I got a call, a young kid, I think, probably horsing around and stuff. You know how kids get a hold of the phone and play when mom and dad aren't looking. The kid hung up after a few seconds, no number or name. You said to let you know if anything came in."

Charlotte had also been picking up on everything the sheriff had missed. Thirty years old, she was a good woman, a good friend. As a dispatcher, she was the best, but even she would admit that as a wife, she sucked.

"No, that's totally fine, Charlotte," he said. "Anything come up on call display, anything to give you an idea of who the kid is?"

The sheriff had picked up on what he was saying, and he seemed to be fumbling for his wallet, so Marcus quickly gestured to the barman to take his keys.

"Nope, nothing. It's likely one of those burners. The kid was young, only said hi and then hung up. That makes me think it's a kid playing around with the phone, you know?"

As he listened to Charlotte, he took in the back and forth between the bartender and sheriff and knew he was going to have to step in. "Okay, could be right," he said. "Just keep an ear open and call me if anything else comes up. Would be ideal to find out so I can check in and at least give the parents a heads-up that the kid's playing with their phone. You know what? I'll pop back into the station."

He hung up and pocketed his cell phone, then saw his sister making her way back over to him, so he tapped the counter and gestured to the pint of stout she'd ordered for him. "Hey, you can finish that," he said. "I've got to go. You done down there, or you going to continue making a fool of yourself?"

Of course, what did she do but roll her eyes? "Oh, Marcus, seriously, keep your opinions to yourself and your nose out of my business," Suzanne said, settling her own stout on the bar top. Marcus just grunted.

Just then, the sheriff stepped off the stool, and he swayed a bit, keys in hand, while Ken held his palm out, demanding the sheriff turn them over.

"Whoa, there!" Marcus said. "You just give those to me. You're not driving anywhere." He grabbed the keys one handed and tossed them to Ken behind the bar, who stuffed them under the counter. He reached for Bert's arm, taking in the concern on his sister's face.

"You got him?" she said.

In the buzz of the bar, he knew his sister understood everything. Just then, asshole Toby came up and joined her, so Marcus just said, "Yeah, yeah. I got him."

But the sheriff pulled away, staggering to the door. "I can drive myself," he said. "I've been driving myself everywhere for longer than you been born…"

Marcus watched a second, listening to the sheriff carry on, then tipped his chin to his sister before following Bert out the door. He grabbed his arm before he could fall over, preparing for the nightly routine: Bert would continue to argue the entire way home, even after he helped him inside the dusty small rancher, put him to bed, and pulled his boots off. He'd be snoring before Marcus left.

Then he'd stop back into the office and check on everything one final time before taking off for the night.

Chapter Two

Marcus worked a piece of gum as he drove back toward the station, taking a second to really consider everything that had happened. With his job, he was the law in this town, running things, making decisions and taking charge. He took in the downtown streets and the passing people that he knew, in a part of the country he loved, surrounded by mountains.

At the same time, this place was filled with secrets, this town, these people, and somewhere out there was the key to the biggest secret of all, the mystery of what had happened to his dad. One day, he knew he'd find answers.

He didn't nod to anyone, though he knew everyone saw him driving past. A wave here, a turn of a head there, even from people he knew had whispered that he'd never amount to anything. Now he was the one in charge.

Marcus took in the bustling parking lot as he drove back past the Lighthouse bar on his way to the station house. His sister was still there, and so was Toby, considering both their cars were still parked side by side in the parking lot. Maybe this weekend he'd take another crack at her, but then again, he needed to remind himself that Suzanne had never listened to anyone when it came to anything. Yup, a typical O'Connell, with a stubborn streak a mile wide.

Suzanne was deceiving. She gave the illusion of being mild mannered and quiet, as the youngest sibling, but that entire personality was a ruse for her rock-hard stubbornness. She did whatever the hell she wanted, contrary to anyone, and she generally got away with just about anything.

Marcus pulled into the spot marked "Sheriff," taking in the setting sun. His stomach growled as he thought back on the possibility of the burger and beer his sister had promised if he joined her at the Lighthouse. Right, not happening now, considering she was preoccupied. Add in the fact that he couldn't stop himself from triple checking things at the station, which he did every night since Peach, God rest her, had left all of them. Nothing was going to blow up in his face at the sheriff's office, not on his watch.

He took in the parking lot, the old brick of the sheriff's office, and the town hall across the street, then made his way up the steps and pulled open the front door. His boots scraped across the old linoleum as he took in the frosted door with "Sheriff's Office" written in fresh black print, something else he'd taken care of.

Inside, Charlotte, the dispatcher, whom he'd known forever, was standing at an old five-drawer file cabinet. Her dark hair was pulled high in a ponytail, and her curves had distracted everyone, namely the male who was cuffed and parked at an empty desk.

"Hey there, Marcus," she said. "You get the sheriff all settled at home?" There was something about the way she spoke, and her smile lit up her entire face and her hazel eyes. Without question, she always stepped in to cover for the sheriff when Marcus wasn't there. Maybe because of that, he'd never been able to understand why her personal life sucked so badly.

"He was snoring Zs by the time I left. You think you can get that friend of yours who cleans houses to stop on over again? His place needs a good going-over. It's a pigsty, and pretty sure there isn't a clean dish or shirt left, the way everything is piled up."

Charlotte paused as she sifted through the files, then stuffed a folder in the already overcrowded drawer. She wore the same brown deputy shirt he did, only he swore it looked better on her.

"You bet I can," she said. "What excuse should I use this time?" She closed the drawer and wandered back over to her desk, which was neat and tidy. He took in the messages she reached for.

"I don't know. What did you say last time?"

She handed him the notepad, covered in her neat penmanship. There were a lot of the same regular nuisance complaints, nothing urgent, all a pain in the ass. When he glanced up, he took in the frown on Charlotte's face, a face that would never get lost even in a sea of pretty faces.

"That he entered some contest to win free housecleaning," she said.

Right, that was easy. "Say it was a package, more than one. Just make up a number, and I'll cover the cost."

She simply nodded, and he knew she'd take care of it. "You know, you don't have to pay it yourself," she said. "Let's pass the hat around. I'm sure both Lonnie and Colby would also pitch in. It's not all on you to look after the sheriff."

What could he say to explain the soft spot he had for a man who'd given him more chances than anyone to turn his life around? Then there was Peach, who had looked the other way when he lifted that pack of smokes. Instead of busting his ass, she'd simply driven up beside him, told him to get in, and taken him back to her place, where she had given him a slice of lemon meringue and some sweetened tea and shown him an old photograph of her brother, who'd done a nickel at Calhoun for theft and was now six feet under, having never gotten his shit together. Marcus had never stolen anything again. That was just one more thing he hadn't shared with anyone in his family.

"That's mighty nice, Charlotte, but let's keep it under wraps for now. Bert just needs a little bit to find his feet again. I can do that much."

Charlotte gave a soft sigh. "You're an absolute gem, Marcus. If only I'd gone with you to prom and not Jimmy Roy."

That was the what-if road, which he had no intentions of going down, considering way back then, Charlotte'd had eyes only for Jimmy. Taking a trip down memory lane was something he wasn't going to do.

"So this is everything for tonight?" he said. "Nothing else has come in?"

She shook her head, gesturing with her chin. "Lonnie is out at the Miller place about a break-in on one of his sheds, some farm equipment taken, and Colby is pulling the night shift tonight, so he's making rounds. No more kids calling for kicks, so you just may be in for a quiet night. Was about to head home myself." She pulled her desk drawer open and lifted out her baggy purse, then rested it on the desk. "Unless you need me to stay and help with anything?"

She was so damn good. Why did she give everything to the job instead of making the tough decisions she needed to with the dickhead she'd married?

"Jimmy still won't leave, huh?" was all he said, knowing there was only so much he could do to avoid the topic. She and Jimmy had gotten married eight years ago and had been separated for seven.

She just shrugged and looked away. She still shared a house with the man she was married to in name only, because neither one of them wanted to give it up. It was pitiful and one of her only flaws.

"What can I say, Marcus? He's as stubborn as me. We're each waiting for the other to blink and walk away so one of us can have the house, but hell will freeze over before I let that man have a house that has been in my family for two generations."

That was why she would never be free.

"Any progress with the lawyers?" He didn't know why he'd asked, as she only shrugged. He wanted to point out to her again, as he had a dozen times, if not more, that she was only making her lawyer wealthy, and she could have bought two houses by now if she'd only walked away.

"He keeps telling me the same thing as you, that it's just a house and it's not going to get me back my last seven years. Do I want to give away another ten, twenty, or move on and be happy? But I'll tell you exactly what I told him: That was my grandparents' house. I love that house and don't want to live anywhere else, so he needs to do his job, get a court date, and get Jimmy the fuck out of my house. Jimmy's lawyer has managed to do everything he can to delay every single thing all because of one mistake I made."

He could hear her frustration, and boy, he felt the bite of her words. She was passionate about that house. He wondered why it was that some women held on to the most ridiculous things, and he thought about his sister Suzanne, too. Thankfully, the phone rang, so he didn't have to think of something inspirational to say.

"Sheriff's office," Charlotte said, without the same sweet voice she normally used. Yeah, there was a side of her that just couldn't be reasoned with.

Whoever was on the other end had her flicking those hazel eyes over to him and snapping her fingers to drive home the urgency and get his attention.

"Honey, can you give me your name?" she said, then allowed the phone to slide away from her mouth. "It's that little kid who called before," she whispered.

Marcus gestured for Charlotte to give him the phone, but she was listening to something.

"I'm sorry, I can't hear you," she said. "Is there somebody there? Someone's trying to hurt you? Where's your mommy or daddy? What…hello?" She held the receiver away. "She hung up again, but I think she said her name is Eva. A young kid, just like before."

Marcus reached for the main phone and slid it around, trying to see the number, but all the display showed was the typical blocked number from a burner cell. Charlotte held out the receiver to him. Something about these calls was now bothering him.

"You know what?" he said. "If you don't mind staying for a bit, maybe call Tulli at the state computer crime lab in Missoula and see if he can find a way back to that number."

Charlotte gave a quick smile—of relief, he thought—and dumped her bag back on her desk. "You bet," she said, once again sounding sweet, nice, likely because he'd just given her the one thing she wanted: a reason not to go home and hang out with the man she was still married to.

Yup, he liked Charlotte. Could even have found himself asking her out a time or two, but there was that little fact that she was still married. Taking her home to her place meant hanging out with her husband, who would likely be doing the same type of entertaining, all because neither could get along, and neither would give up the house.

There was something about relationships that sometimes had him wondering why anyone ever bothered.

Chapter Three

"You know what?" Marcus said, turning from the street toward Colby, the youngest deputy in the department. "Finish up this report at the stationhouse, and tell Charlotte, if she's still there, to go on home and turn the phones over to the main after-hours service. They'll pick up any calls coming in tonight."

He took in the flashing lights of the tow truck just pulling in to retrieve the pickup that had blindsided a Ford Escape at a four-way stop. Apparently, both drivers were confused on who had been there first, and they were still arguing. The scuffle had turned a minor traffic incident into a pain in the ass, with just another asshole he had to write up.

Then there was "the kid," who was working a piece of gum, trying to appear as if he wasn't in over his head. Colby appeared barely old enough to shave, which was likely why he'd forever carry the nickname. He surveyed the scene, trying not to appear scared shitless, doing his best to fill out the deputy uniform with his tall, lanky, boyish frame, as if he had some kind of authority to shut down both these assholes. In the end, Marcus had been forced to step in.

"What about him?" The kid gestured to the asshole with the bloody nose, the owner of the pickup. He seemed to have a history with the other guy, who was still carrying on about the huge dent in the back end of his rusted-out Escape.

"Give them both a ride home. I'll have Wally tow these vehicles out of here, and—" His cell phone rang again. He pulled it from his pocket and took in the office phone number. "Hold that thought," he said to the kid. "Charlotte, you're still at the office? Thought you would've left by now."

"Marcus, that kid called again," Charlotte said. "I've still got her on the line." It was there in her voice, the urgency. The knot in his stomach was so tight as he realized this was the third time the girl had called. "I'll patch her through. Her name is Eva."

"Shit—yes," Marcus said, "and anything else you find out about her, too, like where she is…" he started before he heard the click and knew she was now on the line.

"Eva, this is Charlotte again. Listen, I have Deputy O'Connell on the line, and he's going to help you. You tell him everything…"

"Is he going to come and get me?" Eva said.

Yeah, she was really young—and scared shitless, from what he could tell.

He didn't know why his heart was pounding the way it was. "Eva, are you there? This is Deputy O'Connell. Yes, I'm going to come to you. I just need to know where you are. I need you to tell me everything. Are you hurt? What happened? Where are you?"

Marcus found himself walking toward his cruiser. In an afterthought, he turned to the kid, who had a confused look on his face, and gestured for him to finish up and take care of things.

"I'm scared…" Eva said. She was breathing heavy.

He leaned against the top of his cruiser. The lights were still flashing, and he stared at the houses around them, at the few people looking over to the accident. "Okay, Eva, I know you're scared, but I need you to listen to my voice. I need to know first if you're safe. Can you tell me what's wrong?"

"Yes, uh-huh, I'm hiding…" she said. She had such a sweet voice, but she wasn't telling him very much.

"Okay, Eva, how old are you?"

"I'm six, six years old. Are you a sheriff?"

His heart squeezed at her innocence. "I'm a deputy, which is like a sheriff. Eva, can you tell me where you live? Do you know your address? Where're your mom and dad?"

Okay, maybe he was asking too much. It could be hard to get any information out of a child.

"I don't know," she said. "Can you come and help? I'm scared. I don't want him to hear me."

He could hear Charlotte still patched in. "I'm going to come there," he said, "but I need to find you first. Eva, do you live in town?"

"I don't know."

He shut his eyes as he pulled open the door of his cruiser. "Do you see other houses beside you or buildings? Is it a house or an apartment?" He flicked off the flashing lights and climbed in behind the wheel, vaguely hearing the commotion in the background as he set his cell phone down and connected it to the Bluetooth speaker.

"It's a house," she said. "There's a front door and a big yard."

Oh, great. This would be like finding a needle in a

haystack. "Charlotte, get Tulli to locate this call," he started.

"Already on it," she said. "He's tracing it now. Just keep talking, Eva, and don't hang up this time so we can find you."

"But I have to be quiet," Eva said. "I'm scared of him…"

So the problem was a man?

"Who are you scared of, Eva?" Marcus said. "Is it your dad? Are you at home?"

She whimpered. "No, he's not my dad. This isn't my home. I don't know where I am. It's big and woody."

He silently willed Charlotte to hurry up and for Tulli to do something. "Okay, I just need you to calm down, Eva. I'm going to come and get you, and I'm going to help you. We're looking for you right now. Can you tell me whose phone you're calling me from?"

"It was in his pocket," she said. "He put it on the table. Will I get in trouble for taking it?"

He shut his eyes, wishing he were right there to reassure her. "No, you did the right thing. You are not in trouble. That was really good thinking on your part, calling me, calling for help. Tell me where you are in the house."

"I'm hiding in a back room where there's a bunch of old stuff, but there's just trees outside. It's dark, and I don't remember. I don't know where I am…"

"That's fine, don't worry. I just need you to tell me anything. Do you see any houses around you? You said there's trees. How about a car or truck? Do you hear sounds outside, maybe of cars? Is it close to a road?"

It was her breathing that bothered him, the fact that it was so panicked. She was so damn young, and whoever this guy was, he didn't want him to figure out that she was on the phone with the police.

"Come on, Eva, really listen. Close your eyes and tell me what you hear."

"There's creaking," she said. "I can hear him. He's talking. I can't see anything. Do you want me to look out the window?"

In that second, he realized that moving might put her in danger. "No, don't move," he said. "You said you're in a back room. Is this a bedroom? Are you hiding? Where are you in the house? First things first, I want to make sure you're safe."

"He can't see me. I'm a hiding in the back of the house where the coats are hanging. There's a big table and boxes, and it's dusty. I don't want him to find me."

Okay, it sounded as if she'd found the ideal hiding spot.

"Is there a window there or a door you can see out of?" He was gunning the engine, driving blind, passing a car on the highway who pulled over as he flicked on his light to get around him.

"Over there, but there are curtains," she said. "Do you want me to go over there? I can't reach. It's really tall."

Likely not a great idea.

"No, Eva, you just stay where you are, right where you are. You said this is a man. He's not your dad. Do you know him, or is he a stranger?" Marcus gunned the engine again, wanting Tulli to hurry the fuck up. He was blind on a highway without a clue which way to go, which direction. For all he knew, he could be going the wrong way. He took in the clock on his dash and the minutes that had passed.

"He's a bad man. He scares me. Oh no, I can hear him! He's coming…"

"No, you stay on the line with me, Eva. Don't hang up. You stay right where you are."

The line went dead.

"Fuck, shit!" He slapped the steering wheel, willing this

kid to be okay, wishing he wasn't feeling so damn helpless. "Charlotte, tell me you have something, that Tulli has something."

"Just give it a second, Marcus. I've got Tulli here on the other line…" There was a pause. "He's got it! I've got it. Shit, I'm sending the address to you now. It's in the middle of nowhere, Marcus."

His phone dinged, and he saw the address and knew exactly where that was, likely a cabin. "Okay, I'm on my way. If she calls back, you patch her right through to me."

"You got it, Marcus. Listen, you want me to send Colby out?

He was already shaking his head. "No, the kid's got to run two idiots home, and I don't need to worry about babysitting his ass out here. Call Lonnie, give him the address, and tell him to meet me out here—and for God's sake, Charlotte, if she calls back in, patch her right through."

He hung up as he pulled a U-turn right in the middle of the highway, going back the way he had come, gunning it, knowing he didn't have to tell Charlotte to stay at the office. It was just something she'd do.

At the same time, he couldn't shake this sick feeling, all because of a call from a kid. Worse, this was the one thing cops all knew, that dreaded third call. When it came, they knew it wasn't going to be anything simple. He didn't have a clue what kind of danger this little girl was in.

"Damn it! Please let her be okay."

Chapter Four

Marcus flicked off his headlights, taking in the GPS. He was close, but all he could see were trees along the dirt road. To him, this was just another place in the middle of the woods. His cell phone was mounted on the dash, and when it rang again, he tapped the green button to answer. "What do you got, Charlotte?"

"Tulli is still working on who owns the house. He got the number of the burner, and I've sent it to you. Called Lonnie, too, but he's not answering. Colby called in, said he can come out if you need him to instead of stopping into the station. Or what about the sheriff? May be time to bring him in."

He just shook his head, not able to see shit because of how dark it was. "Sheriff's out for the night. You know that." He knew he didn't have to explain more. She'd know. They all did. He was passed out and in no shape to help anyone. Maybe by morning, but morning was a long way off. "Nope, tell Colby to finish up, and get him to pop into the station. I'll call back if I need him."

He'd just as soon not have the kid anywhere out here,

where he'd need to worry about him, too. He took in his dash, seeing the cell phone number, which was like gold, but he knew he couldn't call it no matter what. The ring alone would give Eva away, and he didn't have a clue what was going on inside the house. He hated being in the dark.

"Do you want me to try to get Eva on the line?" Charlotte said.

"And let whoever that dirtbag is hear her? No, absolutely not, but at the same time, if Eva calls, do whatever you can to keep her on the line, to keep that telephone line open…"

"You know I will, Marcus." There was just something about her soft voice, how much she cared. He was glad she was the one on the other end of the phone, getting what he needed. As he took in how rural this place was, heavily treed, an awful sick feeling grew in the pit of his stomach. He dialed his cell phone and let it ring.

"This had better be good," his brother growled on the second ring.

"Wouldn't call otherwise. Listen, I've got a problem, and it would really help me to have you out here. I'm tracking down a call out in the middle of nowhere, north of the Calhoun place on River Road. There's tons of terrain and not much else. You know where I'm talking about? Kind of place where if it can go wrong, it will."

He could hear a squeak in the background, likely Ryan climbing from bed. He could hear his partner, Jenny, too. Maybe they had been asleep.

"Doesn't sound good," Ryan said. "Yeah, I know that area well, nothing but trouble and everything else. Where exactly are you, again?"

Marcus rattled off the address as he pulled over and turned off his engine, taking in how black it was outside. There was just something about this. He wanted to know more about this house and who was there. Worse, he didn't have any information about the guy Eva was scared of.

"You have any backup coming?" Ryan asked. Marcus could hear what sounded like clothes being thrown on.

"Just you. Listen, I'll watch for you. I've parked a ways back so whoever it is can't see me, so be as quiet as you can, please."

"Who do you think you're talking to?" Ryan said before hanging up.

Marcus would have laughed at the smartass comment if the situation weren't so dire. He climbed out of his cruiser, then reached for his cell phone as it rang again. In the dark of night, the crickets in the silence were creepy, making him feel like anything could be lurking in the shadows.

"What do you have?" was all he said. He had answered on the first ring.

"Marcus, Eva is on the line again," Charlotte said, her voice urgent. "I've patched her right through."

"Deputy O'Connell, I'm really scared. Are you coming to get me?"

He wanted to say he'd be right there. "I'm outside now, Eva. Listen, are you still hiding in the back of the house where you told me?"

"I'm still here, but I'm over behind the boxes now."

He wanted to nod, but there was no point, considering she couldn't see him. "You didn't tell me who the man is. Is your mom or dad there, or is it just the man? Anyone else?" He needed to know what he was walking into.

"I can't hear Mommy anymore. She and Tommy were fighting. She told me to hide, so I ran. I took Tommy's phone. I'm not supposed to use the phone..."

"It's okay, Eva. You can use the phone. You have my

permission, and that is the only permission that matters. You hear me? Is your mommy hurt?"

It was sounding like a domestic disturbance—a boyfriend with a temper? He didn't know. All kinds of things could go sideways at this point.

"I don't know if she is. Can you help my mommy?"

"Yes, I will help your mom, but you tell me about her. What's your mommy's name?"

"Mommy."

He wanted to laugh and would have if the situation weren't so dire. "I know you call her mommy, but listen to me, Eva. Tell me, what do other people call your mommy, her name? Mine is Marcus, yours is Eva…"

"Reine, her name is Reine."

He flicked on his flashlight and hurried down the dark path, seeing that it was a driveway that led to a couple different places. Which path to take? "Reine…that's a nice name. What is your last name, Reine and Eva what?"

Come on, please know your last name. He had to think of what he had known at that age. Of course he had known that he was named Marcus Finnigan O'Connell, and his address, his phone number, his parents' names. He'd known that Suzanne had been a crying baby, and he had a mother and a father, brothers and sisters, a red bike with a bell that he'd ridden everywhere, and a teacher he believed had never liked him.

"Colbert," she said. "My name is Eva Colbert. My mom is Reine Colbert."

Great, they were getting somewhere. He knew Charlotte was in the background, picking up on all this, and she would be giving everything to Tulli.

"This is great, Eva. Just, whatever happens, don't hang up the phone. If you hear him coming, just stop talking. As long as the phone is on, I can hear what's going on in the house."

"Okay, but you promise you're coming?" The plea was there in her voice, an innocent child who was looking to him to save her.

"I'm coming. I'm outside now, but I can't walk in the house just yet. I need you to be my eyes. Can you do that for me, Eva?"

"I can do that, but can't you just come and tell Tommy to let you in?"

He wished it were that simple. "Not just yet. I need you to be brave for me for just a little bit longer. You just stay hidden and quiet as a mouse, okay? You said his name is Tommy. Is there anyone else in the house other than you and your mommy and Tommy?"

"No, uh-uh, just Tommy and Mommy. He brought us here. We were cold."

"So is Tommy your mommy's boyfriend?"

"No, he was helping us. We just met him when we were cold, and he said he knew a place. It was his. He brought us here."

As he stepped around a bend in the narrow dirt driveway, thick with brush, Marcus could see a light and hoped this was the right place. He flicked off his flashlight, seeing what looked like a small cabin. He thought there was an old pickup off to the side, and a shed. In the dark, it looked as if the entire place had been there forever.

"So this is Tommy's place. What is Tommy's last name?"

There was just something about watching the old cabin. He thought the light had to be coming from the main room, but it was darkened by the curtains. He didn't have a sense of what was going on inside.

"Just Tommy. I don't know his last name."

"Okay, listen. Does Tommy have any weapons, any guns on him?" For all Marcus knew, he could have an entire arsenal back there, something else he didn't want to walk into.

"He had a gun. He held it at Mommy, and she told me to hide. He was angry."

An angry man and a gun, not a good combination.

"Any other guns there? Do you see any others in the house, in the room you're in, where Tommy is?"

"I didn't see any. I don't know…maybe."

Didn't help, but best to assume he had more than one. That assumption might at least keep him alive. The dumbasses who didn't assess all the risks were the ones who ended up dead. Just something Bert had drilled into him.

"Okay, Eva, that's really good and really helpful. So how did you and your mommy get here with Tommy?"

"Some stranger gave us a ride, and then we walked from the road. It was a long ways, but Mommy said it would be okay once we got here. But it's not. My mommy's scared. I'm scared."

"So you don't know Tommy? Tommy didn't have a car?" He was trying to piece it all together, a mom and her little girl and some guy who had brought her way out here. None of this sounded good.

"No, he was a stranger, but he was nice. He brought us a blanket where we were sleeping. He didn't have a car, but he said he'd find us a ride, and then Mommy said we were leaving. It was cold at night, really cold. We used to live with these nice people, but we had to move, and we met Tommy… Oh, he's coming! He's calling me. Deputy O'Connell, he's coming…" Her voice was high pitched with fear.

He could hear a man's deep voice, yelling, calling her

name, and he started around the bush to the cabin. Truth time. This was it.

"Eva, do not hang up! You stay on the phone with me…"

He heard her scream. The man had found her. He yelled something at her, and Marcus feared the worst.

"Who the hell is this?" a deep voice barked over the phone.

Marcus could only hope Eva was okay. "This is Deputy Marcus O'Connell with the Livingston sheriff's office. Is this Tommy?" He knew authority was in his voice, but everything about this situation was taking a turn he didn't like.

"What the hell do you want?" Tommy snapped. He wasn't sure what else he heard in the background.

"I'm outside your place right now, Tommy. You have Reine and Eva Colbert inside the house. Is anyone hurt inside?"

Did he even have the right place? The curtain swayed, so there was his answer. He thought someone looked out, and then the line went dead. He stepped over to the truck, which was closer to the cabin and likely hadn't been driven in decades, and shoved his cell phone in his pocket. He moved to unholster his gun.

The front door opened, and a man stepped out, bare chested, with longish dark hair and a pistol in his hand. He held it up and fired in the air. "Get the hell out of here!" he yelled.

Someone shrieked from inside. At the same time, Marcus spotted headlights and thought he heard his brother's pickup in the distance.

"Who the hell is that?" Tommy snapped.

Marcus held his gun, ready to fire. "Just back up," he

said. "Told you, Tommy, no one wants anyone hurt. Just let the girl go, and her mother, and then we can talk."

Instead of saying anything, Tommy looked right his way and lifted the gun. Marcus hit the ground just as he fired two more shots.

Chapter Five

His phone was to his ear, and he kissed the dirt. He was pretty sure Tommy had walked back into the cabin and slammed the door. In that second, Marcus felt as if he was holding the fate of everyone in the palm of his hands. He hadn't fired back when he knew anyone else in his position likely would have.

Ryan answered on the first ring. "What the fuck was that, Marcus? Is he shooting at you?"

"Yeah, he's got a pistol. Listen, don't drive in here. He saw your lights. You see my cruiser, where I'm parked? Stay on back there."

"I parked. What kind of nutjob you got in there? What the hell are you walking in on, Marcus? What's this guy's story?"

Marcus made his way to his feet, crouching down, taking in the cabin, which was dark except for the little light he could see through the curtains. "Just trying to find out. All I know is there's a little girl inside who called 911 for help. Where are you right now? I'll make my way back to you." He was still behind the truck, feeling the bite of the bushes against him.

"Don't bother. I'm already here."

He spotted the flick of a flashlight in the bushes behind him, about ten feet away, and pocketed his phone. Ryan cut through an opening from a path he hadn't known was there. His brother wore a ball cap and his ranger coat.

"What's going on here?" Ryan said.

Marcus holstered his gun, which he'd somehow reached for again instinctively. He could feel his adrenaline pumping as he tried to pull this situation together. "Not sure," he said. Just then, his phone rang with the sheriff's office number. "Charlotte."

"Marcus, are you okay? I heard a gunshot and the line went dead. I think he found Eva in the house. Is anyone hurt?"

"I don't know. My brother's here now. It appears Tommy has gone back into the house. I don't know what's going on inside, but keep trying to reach Lonnie, because I want him out here. I'm going to try getting this guy back on the line and find out what the story is, at least see if I can somehow get the mom and daughter out of the house and out of harm's way. I don't know if this is a kidnapping, a domestic dispute of some kind, or something else, but what I do know is there's a scared little girl in there. Right now, I want you to get Tulli to pull records on this place and find out who owns it, who Tommy is, everything and anything."

"Will do, Marcus. I'll call you right back."

He pocketed his phone and took in his brother, who had picked the perfect spot to eyeball the cabin.

"Well, this isn't sounding good," Ryan said. "You have no idea who this guy is?"

Marcus shook his head, knowing the properties out this

way had changed hands a time or two over the last number of years. They were so spread out and isolated. He didn't know what to say. "No, no idea at all. The little girl is only able to tell me that his name is Tommy, and her mom is inside. It sounds like he brought them here. Don't think the mom really knows him. Something has gone wrong, and now they're both fucked. You familiar with anyone out here?"

He pulled out his cell phone again and pulled up the number for the burner cell. He hadn't wanted to call before because it would give Eva away, but now it was a moot point, considering it was the only way to talk to the guy inside.

Ryan looked around and gave his head a shake. "None whatsoever. Can't remember coming out here for any problems, either, but that doesn't really help you does it? A lot of these properties aren't locals, you know. They're summer folks. But some cabins have been in the family forever and such."

Marcus knew that much, which also didn't help. He dialed the number of the burner cell and put it to his ear. "Guess there's only one way to deal with this: get him back on the phone and talking and find out his story."

His brother said nothing, but Marcus knew he had his back. He listened to the phone ring a second time, then a third.

"What!" Tommy snapped, his deep voice filled with anger and amped-up energy. He was well on his way to ensuring someone ended up dead.

"Tommy, don't hang up. This is Deputy O'Connell. I'm outside and just want to talk. Is everyone okay inside?"

"Did you not get the message? Get the fuck out of here, cop. You're not wanted. You're not welcome."

Okay, so he didn't like cops. That wasn't the first time he'd heard that.

"I can't do that, Tommy. You got a scared little girl in there. Is Eva okay?" He stared at the front door from where he was on the path. Ryan had stepped out a little farther and was watching the cabin as well.

"You think I would hurt a kid?" Tommy snapped.

Marcus wished he'd come outside. He wished Lonnie would answer the damn phone and get out there as well to back him up. More and more as of late, he'd been feeling as if he was the only one running the sheriff's department in a place where it was impossible to be a one-man show.

"Didn't say that, Tommy. I just want to talk to you. Is Eva okay?"

"She's fine, although the little shit took my phone and was playing around with it. She knows better."

He knew his brother could hear what Tommy was saying by the way he dragged his gaze over to him. Marcus couldn't hear anything or anyone in the background. "Look, she's scared. I don't want Eva hurt. I just want to know if she's okay, and her mother. How about you send them both out? The last thing anyone wants is for anyone to get shot or hurt in any way."

"No, I'm not sending them out," Tommy said. "It's late. She should be in bed, asleep. Her mother can put her to bed. Everything's fine here. They're fine. You can go." There it was again, the dismissal.

"Afraid I can't do that, Tommy. You see, as soon as someone calls 911, we have to come out and make sure everyone is okay. How about you let me in the house and let me see that everyone is okay, and we'll all sit down and talk and find out what the problem is, and if it's the case that everyone is fine, then I'll be on my way."

There was also the matter of the gun he'd fired off,

though. Marcus didn't think he was getting anywhere near the story he needed.

"Hey, I'm telling you everyone's fine here," Tommy said. "Reine, what the hell? You keep that little shit in line, you hear me?"

Now he thought he heard a woman's voice in the background.

"Hey, hey, Tommy, how about this?" he said. "You come outside and talk to me and tell me what the problem is in there. Let's talk face to face." He wanted to step out, but Ryan had his hand on his arm and shook his head.

"No, I'm not coming outside. For all I know, you've got someone out there just waiting to take me out with a single shot as soon as I step out, just because. I told you everything is fine here, the girl, her mother. They're fine. They wanted a place to stay. I gave her a place to stay."

He still didn't know anything about the situation, and he wasn't getting any direct answers. "So this is your place, Tommy? What's your last name? We ever met before?" Namely, he wanted to know if he'd ever arrested him, if he'd ever done time. He'd have remembered.

All the man did was laugh, and it wasn't reassuring. "Yeah, I know what you're doing, trying to find out anything you can about me. I did my time, served my country, and this is what I get? I'll tell you what, Deputy. I pay my taxes. I gave everything, but what did I get in return? Nothing. I was just another idealistic, wet-behind-the-ears kid. Didn't understand what the hell I signed up for. But I'm not that way anymore. Now I just want you to leave me the fuck alone."

So he had served—in the military, army, marines, navy? It was a start.

"You were in the military? What branch? My brother's in the military. Sounds like it didn't work out for you?" For a minute, he thought Tommy was going to hang up, but he didn't.

"You want to talk to the girl?" he finally said instead. "She's right here."

He felt that knot in his stomach again as he pictured the phone being passed over to Eva. There was definitely something more to the military angle.

"Deputy O'Connell?" she said.

"Yeah, Eva, I'm right here. I'm right outside. Are you okay?" He shut his eyes for a second and felt his knees weaken.

"I'm okay, but I'm scared."

He wasn't sure what to say. "Is your mom there? Is she okay?"

He pictured Eva nodding, but he could hear Tommy saying something to her.

"You've talked to her, and now you hear she's fine," he said, back on the line. His voice had softened, but he still seemed to be fighting an urgency that Marcus couldn't put his finger on "Now go."

"I can't do that, Tommy. Told you before. She's scared. You keeping a little girl and her mother here when they don't want to be here is a problem. It's called kidnapping," he added, not wanting to push his buttons but also not knowing where the hell his head was.

"Who said anything about kidnapping? I didn't kidnap anyone."

He heard him say something else, but he couldn't make out what it was. Just then, the front door opened, and light spilled out. A woman stepped outside, and the line went dead. He pocketed his phone and moved into the open, closer to the cabin, taking her in. She was slender, with shoulder-length hair, dressed in blue jeans and a T-shirt.

Tommy was in the doorway, one hand on the frame, the other loosely holding the gun.

"Reine Colbert?" Marcus called out and stopped by the truck just in case he needed to take cover.

"Yes, that's me," she said. "Look, I'm sorry about all this. Eva shouldn't have bothered you. We're fine, though."

Something about the way she said it rang false. He wondered what Tommy had said to get her to step out there. Had he threatened her?

"Reine, are you being held against your will, you and your daughter?"

She was shaking her head and rubbed her arms in the cold. He should have been cold, too, but the adrenaline pumping through his body numbed him to it.

"No, we are not," she said. "Tommy here has helped us. It's fine. We're fine, as you can see."

He tried to see into the cabin, to see Eva. Tommy glanced back inside. His brown hair was long and kind of a mess, and he was unshaven.

"Your daughter called me and is scared," Marcus said. "Did you tell her to hide?"

Why was Reine just standing there? Was it to protect her daughter?

"My mistake," she said. "Yes, I did, but she misunderstood. Look, we just needed a place to stay. Tommy brought us here. Everything's fine. This is all just a misunderstanding."

"You heard her," Tommy said. "It's fine. They're fine. Now go on." He flicked his hand and the gun, a motion to leave, but Marcus still couldn't see the little girl.

"Well, see, here's the problem," he said. "I have a 911 caller, a little girl who called in terrified, scared of you, Tommy. Reine, you're trying to say everything is fine, yet here you are,

Tommy, holding a gun. You're telling me this is all some sort of misunderstanding? Well, I'm telling you I'm not leaving. One, you shot off that gun, Tommy. Reine, you're telling me you're fine, but I don't see your daughter. Now, this is the last time I'm going to tell you. Reine, you call Eva outside, and both of you come on down here now, because I'm not leaving when I know a little girl is afraid inside. Tommy, what you're doing right now isn't reassuring me in any way that anyone here is fine. So how about this? You drop your gun, and keep your hands where I can see them. Then the three of us will sit down and talk about what's really going on here," he said.

And what did the man do but laugh?

Chapter Six

"Look, you've got to give me something," Marcus said into his cell phone as he pulled open the door to his cruiser and climbed in. He flipped open the laptop secured to the swivel mount where an armrest would typically be, glad the sheriff had insisted the county fork over the funds to bring their department up to modern times. It was another request that had been put together by Marcus behind the scenes. The laptop gave him access to databases of witness reports, paperwork, and even crime scene photos—everything at his fingertips.

"Look, Charlotte's been riding my ass too, Marcus," Tulli said. "All I can tell you is the facts on paper. The owner of the property is Thomas Marshall, out of Duluth, Minnesota. He owns a shipping company and has a wife, Helen, and two children, Samantha and Thomas Junior. The family appears to be well off. The daughter is married and lives in Florida, and Thomas was in the army and served four years of active duty. Trained at Fort McCoy in Wisconsin, then served in the Middle East, where he was injured. Looks like he was given a dishonorable discharge."

Marcus took in the image of Thomas Marshall, or Tommy, in his military fatigues. There was a warrant out for his arrest for attempted murder. His hair was shorter, his expression pissed. Marcus really had to look to see the resemblance to the man in the cabin now. "I'm not sure it's him, Tulli. You have a last known address?"

"Considering the outstanding warrant? No, nothing. His parents' place in Duluth is the only thing the army has on file for a forwarding address. I can try reaching out to them, but you have everything I do. He's considered dangerous."

Marcus listened to Tulli as he vaguely heard footsteps and spotted a light approaching. Lonnie had arrived and was walking with Ryan. He took in the computer screen, the officer report from Monroe County in Wisconsin. Tommy had beat a man nearly to death with a chain. The images of the victim were gruesome. He was considered dangerous? Well, that kind of went without saying. Add in the fact that he now had a gun in his possession, and Marcus had no choice but to assume the man was deadly. Boy, everything was just getting better and better.

"I don't have anything on Reine Colbert or her daughter, Eva," Marcus said. "See what you can find for me, because there's nothing in the database. Could mean nothing, just that she's never had an incident with the cops. I'm getting the feeling this isn't the kind of story that's going to have a happy ending, not the way this is unfolding."

"Will do," Tulli said. "Listen, I already alerted the sheriff's office in Monroe County about Tommy. You got the sheriff on his way out there as well?"

The last thing Marcus wanted were questions as to where the sheriff was. That was one thing they all knew, how to cover each other's backs.

"Marcus," Lonnie said before he could respond, leaning on the open door. "I talked with the sheriff's office in Laurel. They're sending some backup."

"Great, thanks," Marcus said. "You hear that, Tulli? Just start digging, and get me something I can use to get this guy to stand down and defuse the situation. Better yet, get a hold of his folks. Find out for me what makes this guy tick and what's going on here."

He hung up his phone and closed up the laptop, taking in Lonnie and then Ryan, who was standing at the front of his cruiser, looking up the driveway to the cabin.

"Ryan just filled me in on the situation," Lonnie said. "He's got a gun, and he won't let the woman and girl leave?"

Marcus could smell beer on Lonnie's breath and wondered how incapacitated he was. "Nope, he walked back into the house, told me to get lost, and here we are. I see Charlotte tracked you down."

He was still bothered by the fact that Reine had simply gone back inside the minute Tommy called her. Not a chance he was going in there after him with just his brother and Lonnie there, not until he found out everything he needed to know about Tommy, Reine, and Eva. Too much uncertainty and too much chance for a little girl to end up in the morgue—but then, waiting around, trying to figure out what the hell he was supposed to do wouldn't help either.

"She did," Lonnie said, then shrugged. "Was on a date. Phone was off."

Marcus just stared at him, wondering what he meant by that, considering he was married, with two kids.

Maybe Lonnie could tell from the expression on his face, because he finally said, "Guess you didn't know.

Darlene and I split up. She was tired of being married to a cop."

Right. Well, now was not the time to talk about it. Marcus just shook his head.

"Your call," Lonnie continued. "What do you want to do here?" He pulled out his holstered gun and checked the rounds, something they all did, then re-holstered it. Marcus knew he was waiting for him to say something, but all he could do was walk around to the trunk, where he kept his shotgun and bulletproof vest, everything he needed when things went bad. He pulled the vest over his head and tossed a second one to his brother.

"Come on, vest up, both of you," Marcus said. "Then I'm going to get Tommy back on the phone, get him talking until someone gets me something on him. That's what I'm going to do. It seems there's a warrant out for him in Wisconsin. He tried to beat a man to death with a chain. I think we can assume he has a temper, and he was dishonorably discharged from the army, so who knows what weapons he's got in there? For all we know, the house could have an arsenal, a bunker. Lonnie, I want you around back. Be my eyes back there."

He was walking toward the cabin again, and Lonnie jogged back to his car to pull his own bulletproof vest on. Ryan had said nothing. As he shone the flashlight, Marcus dialed the burner cell again. At least the light was still on inside the otherwise dark cabin.

Tommy answered on the second ring. "What do you want?" he snapped, a man on a short leash.

"It's Deputy O'Connell again," Marcus said. "Told you, Tommy, I can't leave. Just want to talk, is all, and find out what's going on in the house, make sure everyone is doing okay. You okay? How about Reine and Eva?"

"Deputy O'Connell, what are you, the kind of guy who always has to get his man?"

He had his phone on speaker so everyone could hear. "It's not like that," he said. "I need you to send Eva and Reine out. Just let them go."

There was no noise in the background, but Tommy said something in a low voice before coming back on the line. "I'm not sure I can be any clearer," he said. "I'm not holding them against their will. She even told you that. The kid shouldn't have been playing around with my phone. This is my property, so I'm asking you to vacate it now. Leave." He wasn't yelling, but he was quite direct. What was it about his change in demeanor that didn't sit right?

"How about letting me come in there and see for myself that everyone's fine?" Marcus said.

Ryan touched his arm, shook his head. Of course, he didn't agree.

The cabin door swung open. "You want to come in? The door's open, but you leave your gun outside."

Ryan gave another shake of his head and mouthed a very direct no.

"Not going to happen, Tommy," Marcus said. "I need you to come on out and put the gun down, and we'll talk, but I want you to send out Reine and her daughter. Do you want to tell me about what happened in the army? I see that you have a warrant out on you, as well."

This time he heard a sigh, and he couldn't pull his gaze from the open door when Tommy suddenly appeared, wearing a hoodie now, the gun still in his hand. He held up the phone, and Marcus heard the click as he hung up. "It's not how you think it is," Tommy shouted.

Marcus took a step closer to the cabin, his hand

hovering over his gun. He could reach for it in a second. "It never is. Why don't you tell me what happened?"

Maybe he'd be able to reason with him, but he didn't know where Reine and Eva were. He wanted nothing more than to get them out of the cabin. As he moved, he was well aware that his brother was behind him and Lonnie was making his way around the back.

"Thought it would be the answer, you know," Tommy said. "Had a fight with my old man, was never good enough for him, so I walked into a recruiting office. Seems there's one on every street corner. Signed up for the army and bought the bill of goods hook, line, and sinker. Had no fucking idea what I was walking into…you know." He stood on the porch, barefoot, and lifted his arm, brushing his wrist over his forehead. The gun dangled in his hand.

What Marcus was hearing wasn't the answer to his question, but maybe it was the thing he needed to hear. "People never do," he replied. "I've heard it before. My brother's in the military, so I understand what you're saying."

He'd seen enough young ones in trouble who'd signed up, thinking that would be the answer, and next they were AWOL, a few trying to get across the border. Joining up worked out for some, but others ended up quickly drowning, in over their heads. "So what happened? Why'd you leave? You got injured?" He let it hang, recalling the dishonorable discharge mentioned in the file.

"No one ever tells you what to expect when you sign up," Tommy said. "I thought, hey, I'll show my old man, but it was me who got shown instead. Training just about killed me, and then I was stationed overseas, in the Middle East, in every shithole imaginable. Humvee was hit driving over a landmine. I was thrown and lived. Lucky, I guess. Got away with a busted femur and busted head. Expected a medical discharge, but can you believe I didn't get it? The army docs said I'd recover, and they sent me back to active duty as soon as I was on my feet, in a shitload of pain, held together by steel rods. Seems they're short now, so medical discharges are rarer than expected."

He didn't know what to say. "So you returned to active duty," he started.

Tommy laughed. "I think what you want to ask is how I got myself kicked out of the army, living on the streets, with a life as fucked up as mine."

"There's always a story," Marcus said. "Everyone has one. I'm listening—"

Inside, Reine screamed.

Marcus cursed Lonnie under his breath. What the fuck was he doing? He ran toward the cabin, gun in hand, ready, and Tommy yelled something as he stepped back inside.

Marcus was almost there. One more step and he would be at the porch. Everything moved in slow motion as he heard a shot fired, and he instinctively ducked.

When Tommy reappeared, his gun was cocked against the dark hair of a little girl. It was Eva, crying as he held on to her, and Marcus froze, staring into the eyes of a man he knew was completely, one hundred percent unstable.

"Call your man back right now, Deputy," Tommy said, and he heard the click of the safety.

His blood turned to ice, and he prayed in that second that he wouldn't pull the trigger. If he did, he knew Eva's eyes would forever be burned in his memory, the kind of loss he'd never get over.

"Lonnie, pull back!" Marcus shouted, furious. What had he been thinking? He held his hands up, feeling his own gun but knowing Tommy held all the cards.

Tommy lifted the gun and pointed it at Marcus. At

least it was no longer on Eva. "Okay, Deputy, you got your wish. Here's the girl. But guess what? You're coming inside now, so drop your gun and step on up here."

Marcus didn't have to look over to the side of the cabin to know Lonnie had come back out. He would be alone inside. He set down his gun, lifted both his hands, and stepped up onto the porch.

Chapter Seven

Inside the cabin were a small living room with a woodstove, a dated kitchen with a bank of curtained cupboards, and a hallway he suspected led down to where the bedrooms would be. As he stepped in, he heard the door close behind him. He wondered if there was just an outhouse out back or if there was actually plumbing. He doubted very much the place was winterized for the cold that would soon be coming.

"Reine, get his cuffs and bring that chair over here," Tommy said.

Marcus took a second to assess everything. Eva was dark haired, tiny, staring at him in fear. Of course, she was terrified. "You okay, Eva? You listen to me: Everything is going to be fine."

Tommy set his hand on her shoulder, and Eva looked up to him, maybe to see if it was okay to answer. Her shirt was dirty, long sleeved, and she wore red pants and sneakers.

Reine dragged an old wooden kitchen chair over to the

middle of the living room, which also held a sofa and chair so old they must have come with the place.

"Deputy O'Connell, are you going to take us away?" Eva said.

"No, he's not taking anyone anywhere, Eva," Tommy jumped in, giving her a gentle tap on the shoulders, a motion that had her stepping away from him. "Sit on down, Deputy. Reine, get his cuffs."

Marcus took his time sitting in that wooden chair as he took in Reine. Her hair was a mix of red and blond, and she was slender, with a small bust—a little on the too-thin side, he figured, from the way her shirt and jeans hung loosely on her frame. Her eyes were a soft shade of blue, different from Eva's. He couldn't decide whether she was scared of him or Tommy, maybe both. She did, though, reach for the cuffs on his belt.

"I wouldn't do that, Reine," he said.

She swallowed hard and then lifted her gaze to Tommy, who was pointing his gun right at Marcus.

"Don't listen to him," Tommy said. "Deputy, hands behind your back. Reine, cuff his hands to the back of the chair."

"Sorry," she said in a low voice as he put his hands behind him. The cuffs bit into his wrists, and he felt bulked out with the bulletproof vest, which he was grateful he'd had the foresight to pull on. He thought of his gun, lying in the dirt outside, and then he watched Reine as she walked over to the sofa and sat down next to Eva, her arm around her shoulders. They were both shaking, and Marcus took in an old backpack with clothes pulled out next to them and a sleeping bag underneath them.

He knew his brother was likely calling him every name in the book, considering he was exactly where he shouldn't be right now.

"That was quite the low blow there, Deputy," Tommy said. "You wanted one of your men to sneak around to the back and, what, take me by surprise? Maybe you planned for him to shoot me in the head when we were having a nice, polite conversation. Dishonest, dishonorable. Good thing there's no back door. You just showed me who you really are. I don't like it when I'm lied to." He flicked the safety back on the gun and tucked it in the front of his jeans, which were too loose and baggy on him.

Marcus wondered exactly what had happened, considering he'd heard a scream. He turned to Reine. "That was you who screamed?" he said, though of course it had to have been.

She flicked her gaze from him to Tommy. "I did. Just saw a man sneaking around out back. He had the window open and was coming in, gun in hand. He scared me. He pointed his gun at me. Why would he do that? I told you we were fine. Look, Tommy just offered us a place to stay, is all. He was just doing something no one else would, helping us out."

He wasn't sure what to make of what she said. "You know, this is going from bad to worse," he replied. "This isn't solving anything. Right now, Tommy, you have an open warrant out for your arrest, so don't start making this worse by pointing a gun at a police officer, not to mention a little girl. Now you're adding unlawful imprisonment. And, Reine, you mean to tell me you're not part of this? You have a little girl to think of. What would she do without you?" He allowed his gaze to fall back to Reine, then watched Tommy stride into the kitchen. On the counter were a few open cans—soup, maybe.

"I, uh...I told you outside we were fine," Reine said. "I'm not sure I understand why you're still here. Eva, I can't believe you called the police! This is all escalating too fast." She gave everything to the little girl sitting so quietly on the sofa. Eva looked so damn scared.

"Reine, he just had a gun to your daughter's head," Marcus said.

There it was, something in her expression that she couldn't hide. A flicker of anger? Maybe. "He crossed a line," she said, though Marcus could see she was still on the fence. "Tommy, don't you ever touch my daughter again. But you…you're not much better, Deputy. Would that other cop have shot me or my daughter? Both of you…"

Yeah, she was angry at him, as well. Damn Lonnie! What the hell had he been thinking?

"I wouldn't have hurt her," Tommy said. "You know that."

Marcus recognized the shame. He knew when a man felt like shit over something.

"I don't know what's the matter with me sometimes," Tommy continued. "I'm sorry, Eva, for scaring you. I just reacted. The gun went off as I grabbed Eva. I was just trying to get him to stop and keep that other cop out of here." He gestured over to Marcus, who said nothing, staring at the gun Tommy had tucked in the front of his pants. He could snap at a moment's notice.

"Mom, you were scared," Eva said. "You told me to hide when he pulled out the gun…"

He took in how close the little girl sat to her mother now, and he still couldn't figure out what to make of the two. Reine looked over to Tommy, who was behind them now, dumping a can into a pot on the old stove.

"I'll heat up the soup, Reine," Tommy said, "and then you and Eva can eat. There's only a few cans of food, some beans, soups, oysters. Not sure how long to make it last, but we'll figure the rest out in the morning."

It seemed Tommy thought Marcus was no longer an issue.

"That's fine, Tommy," Reine said. "Thank you, but I'm not sure how long we'll stay now." She dragged her gaze back over to Marcus, still cuffed to the chair. His cell phone was buzzing, but of course he couldn't answer it.

Tommy only glanced his way. "Persistent, aren't they?" he said. So he understood what was happening outside.

"It would be best if I answered," Marcus said. "Things tend to go sideways when you're holding a cop at gunpoint. You should know that, Tommy."

Reine stood up, looking shaky. "Look, stop this, Deputy! Tommy isn't a bad man. I didn't handle it right. He's done everything to help us, bringing us here. Tommy, you were confused. You pulled the gun when Eva dropped that jar, when it shattered..."

Tommy seemed to pull into himself, and Marcus wondered if he knew what he'd done. "Look, I'm sorry, it happens," he said. "Caught me off guard. I forgot where I was for a second, is all. Reine, you know I didn't mean anything by it."

She inclined her head and crossed her arms. "Seems we have a situation here, Tommy. I know you didn't mean anything when you grabbed me and threw me down." She dragged her gaze over to Marcus and stepped closer, lowering her voice. "He thought we were under attack and was just trying to protect me. I panicked until I saw his eyes, heard his confusion, you know..."

Over at the stove, Tommy was no longer listening.

"Reine, listen to me," Marcus whispered. "The keys to the cuffs are in my right pants pocket. I need you to pull them out..."

But all she did was walk over to Tommy and rest her hand on his shoulder before she continued. "Tommy found me and my daughter. We were sleeping in a camp under a bridge in Missoula, in a tent, hungry and cold. Tommy saw us when he showed up with food for the thirty of us who were there. We hadn't been kicked out by the cops yet. It wasn't all that safe. My shoes were stolen our first night there, and so was my only winter coat, but we had a tent, at least, some sort of shelter. It had a hole in the top, but if you stayed to the left side, you'd be fine if it rained. We'd been there only about a week…" She crossed her arms, and he was sure her slight stature was from all kinds of hunger. Even her cheekbones were too pronounced She glanced over to Tommy, who was watching her now in a way that showed he cared.

"You were homeless," Marcus said.

Reine shrugged. "Lived the American dream once. If you'd told me, growing up, and even before I married Eva's father, that I'd be living on the streets one day with a six-year-old, I'd have called you crazy. The American dream bit me in the ass. My husband was a firefighter. We had a house in Missoula, small, modest. Eva was six months old when he was diagnosed with lung cancer. He fought it for one valiant year, and then the insurance started denying medical coverage here and there, especially for any experimental treatments. He smoked when he was fifteen, so they called it a pre-existing condition, found a loophole, you know. As a fireman, he was in and out of burning buildings, breathing in all kinds of toxic chemicals. He died five days before Eva's second birthday.

"Then the bills started coming in, a thousand here and there, a second mortgage before my husband died, a third a few weeks after. I had a job, but when you add in paying for daycare for Eva, there wasn't enough. I started selling things off, the furniture, the TV, which we didn't need anyway, as the cable was the first to go. When they shut off the power, I knew things were dire. Four years it seemed I was underwater. Couldn't make enough to feed us, pay the mortgages, and pay back the medical bills for my husband. You know, I even went to the chief, swallowed my pride, sat in the chair across from him and begged him to help and do something about the insurance company. They had denied my husband medical care because they wouldn't wait for their money, and now the hospital had to be paid. But there was nothing he could do.

"We lost the house. The bank came in one day and took it all. I had sold my car long before, as I couldn't afford the insurance payments, anyway, yet I still owed money on it, and then there were taxes I still had to pay. We rented a small suite in the basement of a house, from nice people. Then the hospital managed to get my salary garnished. Do you know by law it's limited to twenty-five percent so you can still pay rent and live? But they made a mistake and took it all. Who was to blame, the courts, my employer, the hospital? It didn't matter. Try getting money back when you have nothing to make them give it. So I went to my employer, T&L, the huge department store chain. HR said they'd look into it.

"When it came time to pay rent, the couple were nice enough the first time, but the second, not so much. I stopped sleeping from the stress of it, and then I screwed up at work because I was so damn tired. I cost the company a lot of money, and they weren't as forgiving. I lost my job. A few days later, we lost the suite. That was the first time in my life that I found myself homeless, wondering how in the hell I had got there. I was one of those people who had locked my car door in parts of town where the homeless lived. I thought they'd done something to deserve such a fate. I saw them as less than people, as drug dealers, addicts, drunks, the lowest of the low. Boy, did I have that wrong."

He didn't know what to say. He took in the mother standing there and realized Tommy was giving her everything, giving her sympathy. He could tell he cared. He knew well that her story was not unique in this country. "I'm sorry, Reine. That's a shitty thing to happen."

She shrugged again. On the couch, Eva was looking to her mom for help. His heart went out to both of them.

"But this here…" he said. "What's happening now isn't the answer and isn't going to fix this situation. In fact, Reine, this could end up going badly for you two. You have a little girl over there who needs you, and yet here you are, acting as an accomplice."

She glanced over to Tommy again, now with fear.

"Then there's the matter of Tommy and the warrant out for his arrest," he continued, and he didn't miss the alarm in her expression. She didn't have to say anything. He could see she hadn't known.

"Is this true?" she said.

Tommy ran his hand over his brow, over his face, then rested both on the counter, his head hanging. He shook his head.

As Marcus waited in silence, hearing the stove tick and the pot boiling, Reine dragged her gaze back over to him. There it was, the minute she realized she was in way over her head.

Chapter Eight

On the counter in the kitchen, Tommy's phone rang, lighting up a like a five-alarm fire.

"Answer the phone, Tommy," Marcus said. "Because if you don't, they'll start to think the worst outside, and that's when people start getting hurt."

Reine gestured to Eva to come over to her and held out her hand. When she did, she held her in front of her, her hands over her shoulders, and took a step away from both men. "Tommy, answer the phone, or let me answer," she said. "He's right. This has to stop before someone comes in here firing. My daughter is the one who's going to get hurt."

Tommy just stood there, staring at the phone.

Finally, Reine left Eva by the door and hurried to the cell phone, reaching for it. "Hello?" she said. He could see her wariness had taken a turn to a point that he hoped would have her walking out of there with her daughter. "Yes, he's right here... Reine Colbert."

It was a one-sided conversation.

"Reine, put it on speaker," Marcus called to her.

Tommy just stood there, then reached for two bowls before he turned off the stove and poured out the soup.

Reine pulled the cell phone from her ear and pressed the speaker button. "I've put you on speaker now."

"Where is Deputy O'Connell right now?" said Lonnie. That dumbass… Marcus would need to pull him aside and have a sit-down with him after he was out of there.

"I'm right here, Lonnie. Who's out there with you?" he called out.

Tommy glanced up and over to him, his hazel eyes unsmiling. There was something else in them that Marcus couldn't put his finger on.

"I'm here, Marcus," said Ryan. "Is anyone hurt in there?"

He didn't miss how worried his brother sounded. At the same time, knew he'd likely have a few things to say to him once this was done.

"Everyone's fine," he said. "My gun is outside. I'm cuffed to a chair right now in the living room. Eva is by the front door, and Reine is here with me now. So is Tommy. Look, Lonnie, I never told you to go into the house. I asked you to watch the back. Doing what you did could have killed someone, and now we're back at square one. What the hell were you thinking?"

There was silence for a second.

"Seriously, Marcus, you're lecturing me? I saw the woman and the window. There was an opportunity. If she hadn't screamed… You know she's aiding and abetting."

He shook his head. Reine's jaw slackened at the spin Lonnie was putting on this. She could be looking at hard time, whether or not this was justified.

"No, Lonnie, it's not as you think," Marcus said. "She thought you were going to hurt her and her daughter.

Keep a cool head, would you? No more going off half-cocked, you hear me? Ryan, you make sure he stays put."

"Look, the sheriff and deputy from Sweet Grass County just pulled in out here," Ryan said. "Charlotte called them in for backup. What do you want me to tell him?"

All he could think was that he was glad his brother was out there. He knew Frank, the Sweet Grass County sheriff, could use a heavy hand when a lighter touch was needed. He was by the book, still operating in a mindset from thirty years ago.

"Just get everyone to cool their heels and not do anything stupid like charge the door or come in shooting," Marcus said. He thought he heard his brother swear under his breath.

"Hey, listen," Ryan said. "Tulli spoke with Thomas Marshall, Senior. We have his number. Apparently, they haven't talked with Tommy in years. He's on his way out here. Tommy, if you're listening, your dad said he's going to do everything he can to help you."

Tommy lifted his gaze to the phone Reine was holding. Everyone was staring at it as if it held all the answers. Marcus didn't miss the confusion on Tommy's face as he strode over and ripped it from her hands, then threw it at the wall, where it shattered. Reine screamed, and a piece of the plastic hit Marcus in the cheek. Reine had Eva in her arms again.

"Tommy, you need to stop this!" she screamed. "You're scaring us! Why would you do that? Your father wants to help you…" She was looking to the door.

"The only person that man wants to help is himself," Tommy said, jamming his hands in his hair and pacing. "That is absolute bullshit."

Marcus didn't miss the fact that the gun was still on the

counter. "Why would you say that, Tommy?" he said. "Look, that was my brother on the phone, and he wouldn't lie about something like that. Whatever differences you have with your father, they are just that. When push comes to shove and your back is to the wall, families tend to put aside their differences, you know, and step in to help out."

Tommy was shaking his head. "Not my family, not my old man. The only thing he ever concerned himself with was making more money, even though he had more than enough. Then there were the women, the booze. Everyone said we were the picture-perfect family… If they only knew. It makes no sense that he would come. The only reason would be because of this shithole cabin that he never uses. He only cares about things."

Reine was staring at Tommy, holding her daughter. Then she dragged her gaze over to him. He needed her out of there now.

"Listen, you have me here now," Marcus said. "Let's wait for your dad to come, and we'll talk. You'll see. Sometimes people change. I mean, how many years has it been since you've seen him? A lot could've happened, you know. Look at you. I bet you're not the same person you were five years ago, or ten." He was doing everything he could think of, feeling the bite of the cuffs and the cramping in his shoulders.

"Reine, you should go eat the soup I heated," Tommy said. "Eva, go eat."

"You know what? How about you let them go?" Marcus said. "My brother out there will see to it that Eva and Reine get something to eat. Reine, take Eva out of here."

She nodded. Maybe he was getting through to Tommy, who, it seemed, was struggling with his own demons. As she put her hand on the door, she glanced back, maybe to see if anyone would stop them.

Marcus held his breath, waiting for Tommy to do something. Then he gestured toward the door with his chin. "Open it, Reine, but stay back until I tell you it's okay."

She pulled the door open, her arm around her daughter, and stepped back.

"Ryan, this is Marcus," he called out. "Reine and Eva are coming out. Make sure no one does anything stupid. They're hungry. Get them some food, blankets."

Tommy dragged his gaze over to Reine and the door.

"Send her out," called Lonnie from outside, and Marcus gestured for them to go.

"Reine, hands up in the air as you walk out. Eva, keep walking. My brother is out there. You'll both be safe," he said, then watched as mother and daughter walked out. He heard shouts.

"Get your hands up! Keep them where we can see them!"

Reine screamed, he thought, and he saw a man in a uniform run and grab her, pinning her down on the ground. At least she was out of there.

Tommy kicked the door closed before he could see more, and then he stood there, looking up at the shiplap ceiling, the same as the walls. He turned to Marcus. "So now it's just you and me, cop. What do you want to talk about? You want to hear about how my father would use his fists when I didn't live up to his expectations, or the fact that we lived in a nice house and had a nice car and any material thing we could want, or the fact that my dad had a mean streak and the only things he loved were his company, his bank account, and his business partners?"

He was seeing a different side of Tommy now, and he knew the man wouldn't need much more pushing before he went over the edge.

Chapter Nine

It wouldn't have taken a genius to figure out from the lights flashing outside that there were more than a few dumbasses out there, guns drawn, waiting for something. If they came through the door, there was always the possibility he could get shot. He just hoped his brother would be able to reason with the sheriff from the county over and keep Lonnie under wraps. Then there was Bert, whom he could picture passed out cold. If there were a time for him to pull it together, it would be now.

"That was good thinking on your part, Tommy, letting Reine and Eva go," Marcus started.

Tommy dragged his gaze back over to him, and he could see the anger simmering there. It was the kind of rage that built, and when it came out, it usually resembled fireworks.

"They weren't hostages," Tommy said. "Why is it that you don't or can't listen? Typical cop. You put a story together, and does it really matter if it's true?"

The way he said it had Marcus reminding himself to tread carefully.

"See it from my point of view, Tommy. You had a gun. A little girl called in three times for help. She was terrified of you. The gun alone was a threat. I asked you to let them go, and there was every indication that they couldn't leave. I asked you to put the gun down, and you wouldn't. But it's all moot now. They've left, so yes, it is just you and me here, Tommy, and you've cuffed me to a chair. It's time to end this. The charges against you are bad, but it could be worse."

Much worse, he thought, with him taking a bullet or dead.

Tommy just walked back into the kitchen and dumped the two bowls of soup into the sink. The gun was still on the counter. From the look of him, Marcus wondered when he had last brushed his hair.

"You know, the minute I saw Reine with her little girl in that camp, I knew they wouldn't last," Tommy said. "Not that anyone chooses to live on the street, but most folks there are doing their best. Shelter, food, and staying warm. Those are the kinds of the things we fought for, yet here we are in a country that won't even look after its own. On the streets, you're trying to figure out where to sleep, if you'll be robbed in your sleep, or raped, or killed. Yeah, there's bad people out there, but most watch out for each other. Then there's the cops."

The contempt was there in the way he said it, but at the same time, Marcus knew that cops didn't willingly go in and move out and harass the homeless. It was always an order from the top, someone behind a desk, a politician, someone in charge.

"I saw her and her kid," Tommy continued, "and I knew my dad's place was here. I brought her and the kid, and I planned on leaving them, letting them stay. It's a roof, at least. I'd get her some food and then leave, because

The Third Call

I can't afford to stay too long in one place. I know how to hide well. At least the army taught me one thing I can use, but that's not saying much."

He had his back to Marcus, then slowly turned around and faced him. "You know, there was a canine unit in my battalion, dogs that they train and use. They send the dogs in first, and most of the trainers are good. They love those dogs. But there was this one guy…everyone knew who he was, a captain. He never should have been in charge of that unit. He was given one of the dogs, a gorgeous sweet shepherd, Sadie. He was a mean son of a bitch. He'd beat that dog when she didn't do what he expected.

"No one said anything, but I did, right to his face, and I got myself written up. He kept that dog chained, kicked her. No one had the balls to stand up and do anything. The other shift would treat her differently, but then she started to bite, turned mean. I knew why. Who wouldn't be mean, when you expect to be hit or kicked? So I went there one night to check on her. I had submitted a request up the chain of command for the dog, because I wouldn't be a good little soldier and do as I was told, but they said she belonged to the US Army, and the request was denied.

"She'd been beaten yet again. I found her in her kennel, bloody, whimpering. There was the captain, too, storming my way, yelling at me to get the fuck out of there, saying I'd find myself locked up and court marshaled. He warned me to stay away, and there I was, disobeying a direct order from him. He had all the power, everything on his side, and he wasn't above using it."

A sick feeling rose in Marcus's chest. He didn't like where this was going, and he didn't think he wanted to hear Tommy say it.

"There was a chain lying right there," Tommy said. "I could tell he had used it on the dog. Her blood was still on it. I was blinded with rage, so much that I couldn't breathe past the tears burning my eyes. I don't remember picking up the chain, but my hand was on it, and I just started swinging. I hit him over and over and over, again and again. He was on the ground, and blood splattered all over me. I would have killed him. Thought I'd killed him, too, as he lay there, bleeding and unmoving.

"I dropped the chain, and the only reason I knew he was still alive was the moan he made. I opened the kennel and lifted the dog out, and she whimpered, and I knew she was still alive. I carried her out of there and walked over to my car, and no one stopped me, but I passed more than a few who were shocked at how I looked. I put her in the back seat of my little compact and drove off that base and into town, just driving until I found a vet. The door was locked, but the veterinarian lived upstairs. He let me in. I carried her, trying not to hurt her any more. We laid her on a steel table in the exam room, and she died not long after."

Marcus shut his eyes, that sick feeling welling in the pit of his stomach. He wanted to vomit. Kids and animals were the most vulnerable. As he opened his eyes, he took in Tommy, who was staring at the gun on the counter. He felt such empathy and fury at the same time, considering it wasn't so black and white after all. He felt his anger.

"The vet said it was a blessing. He didn't know how she was still alive when I brought her in. Her back was broken, her legs, the internal injuries…" He lifted his hand and stopped talking, and Marcus knew the man was numb, still in shock from something that was beyond cruel. He watched every motion Tommy made, the way he shook his head and balled his fists. "She was innocent. She didn't have a choice, being a dog. Can you imagine…?"

He pulled in a deep breath and gave Marcus everything as he reached for the gun, and Marcus felt his heartbeat kick up. His heels were on the ground, ready to launch at him, chair and all. He didn't know what Tommy was thinking or what he'd do.

"I can't imagine, Tommy," he said. "So is that what this is about, the charge of attempted murder?"

There it was, a smile that wasn't a smile. "If you're asking if I'm sorry, the only thing I'm sorry for is that I didn't finish off that fucker. The wrong one lived."

What could he say to reason with this man? He couldn't justify for himself the kind of evil that lurked in some. "The law doesn't always work," he started, "but mostly it does. I understand that these are extenuating circumstances. Tommy, a judge would listen to this and take it into account…"

"You understand what, exactly? How a bunch of people can look the other way? Some said to report him, and others said to follow the chain of command. Others said they were working on it. Others said standing up to him would come back on me, and even if I got something to stick, it was just cruelty to animals, a few thousand bucks and a slap on the wrist. You forget who he is, how the military is. You don't take on the military and win. How is that justice? He was a captain, a shitty one, but still above my pay grade. I was supposed to follow his orders or get totally fucked. But hey, look…" He gestured with his arms wide open, and Marcus took in the wild look in his eyes. He wondered now where he'd heard about the charges against him.

"You've been on the run a long time," he said. "I empathize, Tommy, I really do, and I don't think you've been given a fair shake in the matter. You're right. That shouldn't have happened, but it did. Whatever happens, you have to face up to it. I'll do what I can to help. You have my word."

He'd talk to Karen, his sister. She was a good lawyer. He knew the charges were pretty bad, though, considering Tommy had also been on the run. Then add in the gun he was holding, and the fact that he had trapped Marcus in there.

Tommy opened up the gun, and he was so close that Marcus could see the chamber was empty. Then he walked past him to the door.

The horror Marcus felt had him yanking at his wrists, trying to break free. "Tommy, do not do this! I swear to God, Tommy, there's a way out of this. This isn't over…"

He was still shouting as Tommy pulled open the door and gave him one last look. All Marcus could do was jerk on the chair, and somehow he was up, the chair lifting with him as he bent forward, but he was too slow. He watched as Tommy lifted the gun, stepped out of the cabin, and pointed it out.

Gunfire followed.

"No!" was all Marcus could get out as he leaped forward through the door—but he could see it was already too late.

Chapter Ten

"Marcus, drink this," Charlotte said. She was fussing as she tucked a blanket over his shoulders and held out a steaming coffee in the lid of a thermos.

He leaned against the side of the ambulance and took in the scene around him, seeing the worry in her hazel eyes. He took the coffee that he didn't want, and her hand was on his arm, rubbing. He could sense how upset she was, still feeling the hug she'd given him as she ran to him while he made his way around the body, across the yard.

"You scared the hell out of me, Marcus," she said. "Drink the damn coffee."

He sighed, then forced himself to take a swallow. "You're a good woman, Charlotte," he said.

The sun was coming up on the horizon, offering a little light from the black of night moments earlier. The ground where Tommy had bled out now held just a bloodstain. His body had been tucked into a body bag and put on a gurney, and it was now out of sight in the ambulance. He hadn't been able to say two words to Frank and his deputy or to Lonnie, knowing they had pumped bullets into a man whose gun hadn't even been loaded. Maybe that was why they were giving him space.

"Marcus, you should let someone take a look at that," Ryan said as he strode over.

Charlotte was touching his arm again, the spots above his wrists, which were raw and scraped and bloody from where he had tried to rip his hands from the cuffs. He still didn't know who had uncuffed him after he landed on the wooden porch just outside the door. Maybe that was why his shoulder was aching the way it was. He knew the chair had broken, but everything was a blur. He remembered only hands on him, pulling him up as he stared at the man lying there, unmoving—the worst possible outcome.

The only thing he had seen as he walked away was Charlotte running to him. He'd caught her and held her, and she'd hugged him, all the while fighting tears. So there was that.

"They're fine," Marcus said. "I'm fine. Stop worrying about me."

"Well, that's kind of hard after hearing you found yourself taken hostage, with a crazed man holding a gun at you," Charlotte said. "You could have been killed, Marcus, and then what would I have done?"

If this situation hadn't been so dire, he would have smiled in amusement, but passions, tempers, and everything were now running higher, and he'd have been the first to admit his head was far from clear.

"I'm okay," he said. "You know it would take a lot more to take me out."

With the look she gave him, he was sure she wanted to smack him. He knew she cared, and so did he. Maybe that was their problem.

"Don't joke about something like that, Marcus, not to me. You do everything for everyone. So when does someone get to look after you for once? Just take a minute; give me a minute here with you."

He could see how rattled she was, and he didn't miss the way Ryan took a step back to give them space. She was touching him again, standing right next to him, and then she leaned her head against his shoulder. Something about this awful moment gave him something to settle into. He leaned over and pressed a kiss to the top of her head.

"You should really go on home," he said. "Not much for you to do."

She still had her head rested against his shoulder, her arm linked with his. "Why would I want to do that, Marcus? I'm fine right here with you."

It would be so easy to say okay. "Charlotte, you've got to leave Jimmy," he said. "You've still got one foot in the door with him."

This time, she did lift her head. "I have left him, long ago. He just won't leave my house. I filed for separation. It's just..." She was so damn stubborn.

"Yeah, it's about a house," he said, and he knew Ryan was doing his best not to listen to them. "I know. You keep saying that, but a house is just that, Charlotte—four walls made of wood. Don't you want to be happy?"

This time, she looked up to him, moving right in front of him, so close anyone would think they were together. He could see so many things in the face of this woman he'd known forever. He knew there was something there, but he wasn't about to let himself act on it, not when she still lived with the man she'd married.

She was the one who had kissed Marcus so long ago, six months into a marriage that should never have been. Jimmy Roy had seen it from across the room. Could he blame him for the sucker punch, for busting his lip? Not really.

"You need to eat something, Marcus," she said. "I picked up sandwiches because I didn't know what else to do."

He just couldn't help himself. He touched her cheek, brushing back the dark hair that had slipped from her ponytail. "You see to it that Reine and Eva got fed? They were hungry. I hope someone had the presence of mind to see that they ate and were looked after."

Ryan was still lingering a few steps away, an odd expression on his face. Marcus knew it well, and he took in the scene, the cops, the paramedics. He'd expected to see Suzanne there, but evidently, she hadn't gotten the call.

"I don't see them here," Marcus said. "Please tell me they didn't see what happened to Tommy?"

Something in Ryan's expression told him there was something else he wasn't going to like. That sick, heavy feeling in the pit of his stomach had left him numb. Charlotte turned, her hand on his arm again, her expression one of angst. Anyone else would have taken a step back, but not Charlotte. She stepped closer as if she could somehow be a voice of reason.

"Lonnie cuffed Reine Colbert and stuffed her in the back of the kid's car," she said. "Colby was just leaving when Social services got here and took Eva."

He just stared down at Charlotte and couldn't believe what he was hearing. This was absolute bullshit. He dragged his gaze back over to Ryan. "On what fucking charges? What the fuck?" he yelled, tossing the thermos lid on the ground. The coffee splashed out. He wanted to put his hands around someone's neck and squeeze. Charlotte had stepped back.

"Aiding and abetting, and child endangerment," Ryan said. "Look, we didn't know what the fuck was going on in there. I'm not a cop, and you know I have no authority. I'm here for you, eyes and ears. You remember we were standing with you when she came out on that porch and said she was fine, and Lonnie said she gave him away when he tried to get in the back. He was pissed about what went down, said she was responsible for it turning into the shitshow it did. Said it looked like she was working alongside him, that she alerted Tommy. Sheriff Frank said to book her. Our hands were tied. If it didn't go down that way, then you can straighten it out. Voice of reason, Marcus. I get it, but from the outside, it didn't look as if this was all that cut and dried."

Ryan's hands were shoved in his coat pockets, and Marcus could see none of this was sitting right with him, either. Then he spotted Lonnie talking with the other cops, running his hands through his hair, managing the crime scene, which was something he should've been doing.

He stepped away from the ambulance, letting the blanket fall. He felt a hand on his arm and knew it was Charlotte as he started toward Lonnie, really digging into each step.

"Hey, what the hell do you think you're doing, arresting Reine Colbert?" he shouted. "She's a victim here! And sending her kid into social services?" He took in their faces as he strode toward them. Ryan was beside him too now, his hand on his shoulder, but there wasn't a chance he was stopping him. He grabbed Lonnie by his vest.

"Marcus, what the fuck? Let him go!" Ryan yelled.

He wasn't in any state of mind to be reasoned with, though. He was gutted by everything that had happened. "You son of a bitch!" he yelled. "You really fucked up…"

Everyone seemed to be pulling at him, trying to break his hold, but he'd be damned if he let go.

Lonnie was furious. "The hell she's a victim! I was the one trying to get in and save them. She outright refused and instead gave me away, which put the kid in danger. I have a mind to add a bunch more charges."

"Total, absolute bullshit, Lonnie! All of those charges are going to be dropped. I ordered you to watch the back, not to go rogue and do your own fucking thing. You put everyone in danger, escalating this to where a man is now lying on a slab in the morgue. You wouldn't have forced his back to the wall if you'd just followed my orders, and I wouldn't have ended up cuffed to a chair. That's totally on you. His gun was empty, not a bullet in it… I knew it and tried to stop you."

Sheriff Frank stepped in. He was a big man, same height as Marcus, with about twenty years and fifty pounds or so added. "Hey, enough already! She'll get her day in court. This could have been a whole lot worse, and you seem to forget we have discretion over when, where, and to what extent we decide to prioritize and enforce laws. The charges stand unless your sheriff has other reasons they shouldn't. Just where the hell is Bert, anyways?"

"He's not available," was all he managed to get out as he dragged his gaze over to Charlotte and felt her hand pulling on his arm. Lonnie said nothing, and Marcus turned to him again. "And you never did tell me how much you had to drink before showing up here," he started, but Frank set his hand on his shoulder and somehow had him moved back and away from everyone.

"Look, son, I understand you're upset," he said. "I get it. None of this ended the way any of us wanted it, but it doesn't always work out. You know that, especially in situations like this, when there's a gun and heads are far from cool. You seem to forget that everyone here is doing their best. That boy came out of the cabin as a threat, gun in hand. You know there was no way for us to know the gun wasn't loaded. The perceived threat was very real.

"Do you need a reminder on backing up your brothers in arms? I'm acting sheriff here right now, and I gave a direct order. You know how the chain of command works. Sounds to me as if you're ready to hang a fellow officer out to dry. I think maybe you're not clear, and maybe you're confused after having a gun in your face, being held hostage. So let me remind you how things work. I'm not unsympathetic to the woman here, but she had some responsibility, too. Let me ask, who cuffed you? Did she stand by and do nothing? Did she have a gun on her, making her do what she did?"

Marcus just stared into Frank's face, but he said nothing. It was Reine who had cuffed him. Could he lie if asked? No, it would be in the report. He needed to take more than another minute to consider everything, how all of it had gone down. The bleakness of her situation wasn't being taken into account.

"Just as I thought," Frank said. "Take a few days, son, and get your head clear. It'll all work out just fine. The kid's safe now, the bad guy's taken out, and Ms. Colbert will face her part in this before a judge." Then he patted his shoulder and strode back over to Lonnie, whose ass Marcus still wanted to kick.

Chapter Eleven

He didn't know how Charlotte had managed to convince him to leave, but she was in the passenger side of his cruiser now, with a bag at her feet that held the damn thermos and uneaten sandwiches.

He was driving back to town. The moment felt surreal as he thought back on his desperation the night before, rushing out in response to the call from Eva, who had been looking to him to make everything right.

The crime scene techs had taped off the cabin and yard and were photographing everything. The ambulance was just ahead of them, and Ryan was behind. His brother had said nothing more after he managed to steer Marcus to the cruiser and told him to walk away before he did or said something really stupid.

"I'll drop you at the station, and then I'll get a hold of Bert, finish the reports, and try to get a handle on how official the charges are in the system, if she's even been processed," Marcus said. He'd see exactly where Reine was, and Eva. Then there was Tommy and his next of kin. "Oh, shit!" He smacked the steering wheel.

Charlotte didn't pull her gaze from him. "What is it, Marcus?"

He shook his head. "Tommy's father. He's on his way. Then there's the Wisconsin sheriff's office. Did anyone call them?"

"Colby will handle that part. You need some rest."

"Yeah, no time for that," he said, and even he didn't miss the sharpness in his tone.

Charlotte simply sighed the way she did, never rattled by him. "Well, at least take a minute to grab a shower, a hot one, to get your head together, and some food, a change of clothes…"

He was still shaking his head. He could be damn stubborn when he had his mind set on something. "No, I'll change at the office. You go on home and get some rest. I'm sure there's a clean shirt there…"

"Marcus, I swear to God, everything at the station can wait. You walk in the station now, you're only going to be knocking heads with everyone. Take a minute and get your head together. I know you're pissed off, and I am too, but I also know it's not beyond you to start butting heads with Lonnie. Then there's Sheriff Frank. In case you didn't hear him, because I did, you need a plan, something better than going in and knocking heads together to get the charges against Reine dropped. You need me to remind you that your acting superior ordered you to back down? I was there. I heard him. You and I both know none of this is sitting too well, and I agree with you, but let me remind you that you could actually make things for Reine and Eva so much worse."

There was something about the way she spoke. He knew she was right, but he didn't agree. He took in the ambulance in front of him, which was turning right to the morgue, and the sheriff's department, which was straight ahead.

"Marcus, please." Charlotte gestured to the left, where his bachelor pad was, a one-room loft above the Chinese restaurant on main street, only a few blocks from the sheriff's office. "Get showered. I'll make you something to eat while you get cleaned up, and some fresh coffee, and you give yourself a second to settle and stop acting on emotion. Isn't that what you tell me?"

He took in the turn to his place, then the road ahead, which led right to the sheriff's office. He should really take her back there, let her get in her gray Subaru, and send her home. "So you're using my words of wisdom on me? Kind of fucked up, isn't it, Charlotte, considering you haven't heard me yet or listened?"

"Of course I hear you, Marcus. I always hear you and listen to you. My pride is the only reason I haven't done what you've said, even though I know you're right, because then I'd have to admit that every choice I've made was wrong. I know it was. I can see it in your eyes every day. But you know that already. I think you know me better than anyone ever could. Please…" She gestured to the turn. It was there in her voice, in her eyes.

He didn't know why he did it, but he flicked the signal and turned left, seeing the red brick of the building where he lived, then parked. It wasn't a good idea, taking her upstairs with him. "You should go home," he said again, knowing it was just words.

She just opened her door. "And you need a shower and some food. I already told you I'm not going anywhere. You scared the hell out of me tonight, Marcus. When Lonnie called in to the station to say you'd been taken hostage and how dire the situation was…" She stopped talking as her voice caught. He could feel the emotion between them, and she didn't have to say anything else. Her hazel eyes couldn't hide everything that had been left unspoken between them. "Don't do that again to me. Not ever, Marcus."

He knew every bad choice was made in the heat of the moment. He said nothing. Instead, he pushed open his door and climbed out into the early morning light, taking in the quiet street. The sun was just coming up, and Charlotte Roy was standing right there, waiting for him.

So why was this a bad idea? Was it the fact that she was still married, still roommates with a man she didn't love?

Chapter Twelve

Marcus stood under the spray in the walk-in shower, letting the hot water take some of the ache out of his shoulder, which was beginning to stiffen. His bathroom was small, with a single sink and a toilet. It didn't have a bathtub, but that didn't matter to him.

As he considered everything about what happened, he made a mental note of what he needed to do now. At the same time, he was well aware that Charlotte was in his kitchen, making coffee and something for him to eat, and he was still stuck on what she'd said. This dance and attraction he'd ignored between them had lingered for how many years now? A long time.

When the water went cold, he turned off the shower and reached for a thin navy towel on a hook. He dried himself off, feeling the sting on his wrists, and took in how nasty they looked. The bruising was already starting to set in. He ran the towel over his head and then looped it around his waist, then wiped the steam from the mirror. In his reflection, his eyes were bloodshot, and the scab on his face was oozing blood again. He could use a shave.

He grabbed some toilet paper and dabbed at the blood, then dumped it in the toilet and flushed. He ran his fingers through his thick dark hair, then over his face, then shut his eyes and hung his head for a second as he rested both hands on the edges of the sink, trying to understand the shitstorm that had to be cleaned up and everything that still had to be done. So many difficult personalities were involved, people that wouldn't take a back seat to anyone, just like him.

He pulled open the bathroom door, hearing Charlotte humming some tune. She really did have a nice voice, and that alone added something to the dinginess of his one-room bachelor pad. The high-ceilinged loft was built in a warehouse style, with red brick and a window that filled one entire wall. His unmade bed and easy chair had seen better days, but he had a new flat-screen TV.

In the small open kitchen, Charlotte was frying something on the stove, and it didn't seem as empty as it normally did. He breathed in the smell of coffee and took in the woman who was fussing over him now.

"I made you a cheese omelette and toast." She slid a fluffy omelette onto a plate on the butcherblock counter, with two pieces of buttered toast, and then reached for a mug from the open shelf and poured coffee in it. When she pulled open his fridge and took a whiff of a carton of milk, she made a face. "I think you might have to drink your coffee black. Your milk has soured—and you need some groceries."

She dumped the carton of milk into the farmhouse sink and rested the mug of coffee on the small island he used as a table. He was very aware of the towel still looped around his waist, and she wasn't shy as she took him in, letting her gaze wander over all of him.

"You really should have your shoulder looked at," she said.

He pulled out a stool and sat down before lifting the coffee and taking a swallow. "Not bad. Wouldn't even know it needs milk. Maybe the fact that I didn't make it has something to do with it."

She smiled as she pulled open a drawer and brought a fork and a knife over him, resting them beside his plate. She really was giving him the full treatment, but then, he wondered when she hadn't looked after him in the office.

"You don't have to wait on me, you know, but I appreciate this," he said. He picked up the fork even though he didn't think he was hungry, and he forced a piece of the steaming omelette into his mouth. The orange cheese oozed as he took a bite. "It's good."

She drank from her own mug as she walked around the island, then took the stool beside him.

"Did you make yourself something?" He gestured to her with his fork, then took another bite of the perfectly seasoned omelette. Maybe he was hungrier than he'd thought.

"No, I'm fine," she said. "This is for you. Someone has to look after you, Marcus. You spend all your time taking care of everyone else, everything else, and maybe this helps me settle a bit." The way she said it, she suddenly seemed so shy, awkward. At the same time, he was aware how comfortable she was here and with him.

"Hmm," was all he said. He forked a piece of his omelette and held it up to her lips, and she opened and took a bite.

"It's good," she said. There it was, that smile again. "I love you, Marcus, but I think you know that already."

He hadn't expected her to say it. He finished chewing and swallowing his bite of eggs, then lifted his mug and took a swallow of coffee. He remembered how it had felt to kiss her so long ago. Would they always be thinking of that close call? Even he felt some nostalgia and what-ifs, if he was being honest.

"You know I love you too, but you made your choice, and here we are," he said. "You really want to rehash the past seven years when nothing has changed? That kiss sent your husband over the edge. It shouldn't have happened. It never happened again."

She nodded. "You think I don't know that? At the same time, I never should have married Jimmy. I had doubts right until he put the ring on my finger. I never loved him the way I love you. Marcus, I never expected you to turn your life around the way you did."

There it was, the reason nothing had ever happened between them: He'd been young and stupid, headed in a direction that could have seen him behind bars. At least she'd been smart enough to see that.

"And yet here we are," he said. "You're still married to him, and I know you don't need to say it again, that it's because of the house, but the thing is, Charlotte, this dance we're doing is going to be just that until you figure it out and end it with him. Is the house worth giving up another five years, ten? Because I won't wait around forever. Separated is still married. We may not have talked about anything, but here we are."

He wasn't sure what she was going to say. His cell rang from the island beside her, and maybe out of habit, she reached for it.

"It's the sheriff," she said, handing him the phone, and he saw Bert's caller ID on screen.

He stood up from the stool and answered. "Bert?"

"What the fuck, Marcus, you okay? I just got off the phone with Sheriff Frank about the ruckus that went on last night. He just left the scene, and I'm heading out there now. The woman is being arraigned at two, and you still need to get your report in and filed. I've got to talk with the coroner…"

Break time was over.

"I'm on my way back into the office," he said. "Look, this whole thing is a mess. Reine Colbert shouldn't have been arrested. Lonnie completely fucked that one up. She was a victim there, and so was her daughter, who's been taken by social services. Then there's Tommy Marshall. His dad was on his way. Has anyone thought to contact him?"

Something in Charlotte's expression had him pausing. He knew she could hear everything.

"Don't know nothing about him," Bert said. "Look, my car is still at the Lighthouse. I've got Lonnie swinging by to pick me up. We'll sort it out, Marcus. I'll meet you at the office." Then he hung up, sounding as if this would be just a hiccup when it was anything but.

"I'd better get dressed," Marcus said.

Charlotte reached for his arm. "I guess in the commotion of everything, no one thought to tell you. Tulli did speak with Thomas Marshall, Senior, but the truth of the matter is that he decided not to come out."

That sinking feeling in the pit of his stomach was back. "Seriously? What did he say?"

Did it really matter, considering his son was likely now on a steel slab, ice cold under the knife of the coroner, who was counting the bullets that had been pumped into him and determining which one had officially taken his life?

"Oh, nothing good," Charlotte said. "He said his son made his bed, had done everything he could not to follow in his footsteps. He said Tommy basically spat in the face of all authority and said he wasn't worth his time or the extra breath, considering he'd chosen to sign up as a grunt in the army instead of having a position that could have made him great. He said Tommy disgraced them all by beating a superior officer in the army, kissing his life away, and he wasn't about to lift a finger to help, considering the Marshalls didn't have criminals in the family. He basically told Tulli to get Tommy out of his cabin, and he expected our office to file additional charges of trespassing and breaking and entering..." She paused.

Marcus was having trouble picturing a father who would do that to his child. Maybe because of everything Tommy had shared with him, he knew the man had been experiencing a dark night of the soul.

"Not everyone is a good person, Marcus." Charlotte angled her head, and he pulled his hand over his jaw, hearing the scrape, then over his bare chest and the towel that was looped around his waist.

"So whose idea was it to lie and tell Tommy his dad was coming? Just so you know, he didn't believe it. At least now I know why." He started across the room and pulled open a chest of drawers to fish out clean underwear and socks, then dumped them on the bed along with the towel. He stepped into his underwear before turning around to Charlotte. It should have been awkward, but it wasn't. He sat on the unmade bed, pulling on thick black socks, and then walked over to the armoire, his only closet.

"It was Lonnie's," Charlotte said, "but I would have done the same. It was a desperate situation, not the time to tell a man with a gun that his father hates him and his family's written him off. You would have, too, Marcus."

He glanced over his shoulder to her as he shook out a pair of clean uniform pants and stepped into them, then pulled on a shirt. As he faced her, he had to remind himself that maybe she was right, but it was hard, considering how he struggled to cut Lonnie any slack now.

"Marcus, come on," she said. "I know you're angry, and you have a right to be, but you would have done the same thing."

"Fine, you want me to say it? You're right. It just doesn't help the situation. You know Tommy planned to leave Reine and her daughter there in that cabin, to give them that place, a place he said his family never used. It was just sitting there, empty…" He swore under his breath as he buttoned his shirt and tucked it into his pants, then walked over to the old bar table by the front door where he'd dumped his duty belt. It was missing his cuffs, which he knew were still at the scene. Evidence, of course. He pulled it on, taking in Charlotte, who had slid around and was watching him.

"I understand, Marcus. Everything about this was shitty, but that's what life is sometimes, unfair. I know you don't want to hear this, because I can see how torn up you are by it all, and I wasn't in there with you, but the only thing I cared about was that you walked out of there okay."

She had slid off the stool and made her way over to him, and now she was standing right in front of him. Her hand pressed to his chest, his stomach, and he settled his hand over hers. "And I don't care if this sounds cruel, but if there had to be a choice between you being on that slab or Tommy, then I choose him."

He could see it in her face, in her expression: She was truly afraid.

"Maybe that was the wakeup call I needed, Marcus, because I won't lose you," she said. She was so close, and she rose up on her toes. Her hands slid over both his cheeks, and she pulled him closer and pressed a kiss to his lips. It was soft, tender, the kind of kiss that said everything about what she felt for him.

He allowed his hand to brush back her hair, skim over her cheek. Then he pulled in a breath and ran his hand over her arm before stepping away and saying, "We'd better get going."

As he reached for his shoes and the keys to the cruiser, he knew he should say something else. He took in the woman he'd never get out of his mind as she walked over to his easy chair and reached for her coat and bag, and when she turned back to him, he just shoved his feet into his shoes and laced them up.

She was waiting for him to say something, but all he could do was pull open the loft door and hold it for her. After she stepped through, he followed her out and locked it behind them.

Chapter Thirteen

He had watched as Charlotte climbed behind the wheel of her Subaru, and he'd even taken a minute to see she was settled in okay before he leaned in and kissed her, then closed the door, sending her off home to the house she shared with a man she was still married to.

He reminded himself that the ball was in her court, and this could be a one-way ticket to a broken heart—namely, his.

He was making his way up the steps to the sheriff's office when his cell phone rang, and he pulled it from his pocket, seeing that he had three missed calls, too. His mom's name was on the screen now. Of course she'd heard, and he knew she'd be worried. He pressed the green answer button.

"Mom, can't talk right now," he said as he pulled open the front bank of glass doors to the building. "I'm fine. I'll call you later, though." He hoped that would be it.

"Well, that's fine. I just had to make sure you were okay. Would have expected a call, at least, even just a 'Hey,

Mom, I'm okay!' Don't need the entire story, but I did need that much."

He didn't miss the sharp reprimand, even though he was a grown-ass man. She hadn't raised her voice, but she had a way of getting her point across. "Okay, duly noted. Sorry again, but I've only just had a chance to shower and change, and I now have to get back to it. I promise I'll call later." He started down the hall, seeing the doors to the sheriff's office and hearing voices inside.

"Well, you can come by instead. Owen's barbecuing at Ryan and Jenny's, I have Alison today, and Suzanne and Karen have called half a dozen times. Just got off the phone with Ryan. We'll say five o'clock. You don't have to stay long."

His mom was pulling her kids together, because she'd probably heard he'd had a gun in his face and had been taken hostage, and how close he'd come to being the one in the morgue.

"Can't promise, but I'll come when I can," he said.

"Fine," was all his mom replied, and he had to smile as he pocketed the phone, knowing anyone else's mom would likely have been down there already, questioning him until he told her every detail. He saw that both Suzanne and Karen had called as well, but they would have to wait.

He pushed open the door to the sheriff's office, seeing Lonnie and the kid and Bert, who was standing in the middle of the office, holding a mug of coffee, looking much like a man who'd drunk too much the night before. At least he'd put on a clean shirt, but he still hadn't shaved.

"Charlotte filled me in on Thomas Marshall, Senior," Marcus said. "Has anyone contacted him and his wife again to let him know his son is now dead?" He stepped into the bullpen and around Lonnie, not missing the way he eyed him over. Of course, he still wanted to go a few rounds with him and find out what the fuck had been going through his head.

"I did," said the kid. "I called him. Kind of expected him to let us know what to do with the body after the coroner releases it, but he just said thanks and said to call the military and get them to take care of it."

He just stared at Colby, who he could see had likely hung up instead of pressing for more. "Did he miss the fact that Tommy's not in the army anymore? He was dishonorably discharged. The military will do squat. Call him back again. Tell him to get his ass out here…"

Bert took him in and gestured toward him. "I'll talk to him," he said. "Get me the number, Colby."

This was the reasonable Bert, whom he hadn't seen in a long time.

Bert winced as he looked back at him. "You okay there, Marcus? You get checked out by a medic?"

He took in the sheriff and dragged his gaze over to Lonnie, who had his arms crossed and looked like shit, but at the same time, he seemed to be standing his ground. "I'm fine," he said. "Just bumps and scratches. So where exactly is Reine Colbert right now? Because I told you already she was a victim there, her and her daughter. I want her released." He didn't pull his gaze from Lonnie, who seemed to really settle into his stance.

"She's been charged, booked, and is settled into a cell at County," Lonnie said. "There's no way she's walking."

Marcus found himself taking another step until he was right in Lonnie's face. "And how much did you have to drink before you showed up on the scene?"

Lonnie didn't say anything for a second. "A couple beers, no more than you've ever had before showing up at a crime scene. I was sober and fine."

"You've got a lot more going on than that," Marcus

said. "Your personal life is in the toilet. You split up with your wife and are dating someone else. I'm pretty sure I told you to hold your position and watch the back of the house, but you screwed up. You scared the shit out of her, the way you went all cowboy. You could have gotten everyone killed. When push comes to shove, Lonnie, your reckless behavior is going on the record—"

"Hey, stop this right now!" the sheriff cut in and put his hand on Marcus's chest to make him step back. He wasn't a tall man, but he could stand his ground. "No one is doing anything. Marcus, in my office. Now."

The way he said it made Marcus pull his gaze from Lonnie, who wasn't about to back down.

"Marcus!" This time, the sheriff barked at him in a way he hadn't done in years, so he made himself take a step back. "Lonnie, go on home and clean up. Don't come back until you get some sleep, food, and coffee into you."

The kid stood a few feet back, saying nothing, as Lonnie stepped past him to the door and started out, but not before smacking the cabinet beside him. The noise jolted everyone. Okay, so he was pissed, too.

The sheriff only shook his head and then leveled that serious look back on Marcus. He gestured to his office, and Marcus had to force himself to follow him in and close the door behind him.

"Look, Bert, Lonnie completely fucked up," he started.

The sheriff just held up his hand calmly and gestured to a wooden chair as he walked around the big old desk and sat down. He gestured again until Marcus finally decided to sit.

"I hear you, and I agree," Bert said, "but I've been doing this a long time, Marcus…"

"Bert," he tried to cut in, but the sheriff lifted his hand again.

"Hey, let me finish. Calm yourself. You've been through a tough night, with a gun in your face, a bad situation, getting caught in the crosshairs and cuffed to a chair. Regarding Tommy, you don't get a say in the matter. The law is the law. You can't be pulling a gun on a cop—end of story. No one there could have known in the heat of the moment whether it was loaded. You know that. It's tragic, but that boy had a death wish, and there was nothing you could do. No one is at fault except that boy. Look, I've talked to Frank and Lonnie. I know what went down, but let me ask you this before you finish your report. When you were taken hostage, did Reine Colbert try to intervene, try to help you in any way?"

What could he say to that? It wasn't that cut and dried. There was more to it.

"Did he have a gun to her head?" Bert said. "Was he holding her hostage there?"

No, but at the same time, he'd had a gun to Eva. Tommy had panicked, he knew that now, but still.

"She was scared, terrified," Marcus said. "He was just providing her with shelter, a place for her and the kid. I suspect he had some psychological issues, PTSD. It scared her and started this whole thing, from what she said. She was just trying to survive with her kid."

"Well, she'll get her day in court, and remember, the DA will have final say. Last I heard, she's up on a number of charges. She'll get a lawyer to plead her down, but she's going to do some time. You know that. I know that. You're also talking about hanging one of our own out to dry."

When Marcus took a breath to speak, Bert shook his head again and lifted his hand. "Let me finish, Marcus. You're a good man. I know you've been covering everything here for me for a long time, and you'll always have my gratitude for that, but at the same time, you know there's one thing that can get a cop fired, and that is insubordination. Frank told you to stand down, and now I'm telling you the same thing. Let it go with Lonnie and leave it with the courts. Ms. Colbert will do her time, and her kid is somewhere safe, being looked after." Bert swiveled in his chair and faced the window as the sun poured in.

Marcus wondered how he could say all that. "You really think social services is doing the best thing for that kid? Safe, really?"

The sheriff swung back around to him. "She'll get a roof and three square meals," he said. "Marcus, I've got plans for you. I'm stepping down as sheriff and want to throw your hat in the ring."

For a second, Marcus wasn't sure he'd heard right. The sheriff leaned forward in his bulky frame and rested his arms on his desk.

"You want me to be sheriff?" Marcus said.

The old man took a second to consider something. "I do," he finally said. "That's why I'm telling you to drop it, let it go. There's a bigger picture, Marcus, and whether you want to admit it or not, Ms. Colbert had some responsibility in what happened. I want you to take over as interim sheriff. I'll cite health problems. It'll be fine with the council, and I'll grease them up and say all the right things, and then you can run in the next election. But remember, folks don't like scandals, especially in their police department. You're the hero right now, so take a word of advice. Don't make Lonnie look like the bad guy, or you will lose." Bert gestured to Marcus, and he knew then that he wasn't going to be able to convince him to set the record straight. "So go on, finish up that report, and get it over to the DA for the woman's arraignment this afternoon. Then take a few days off and get your head together."

That was all the sheriff said.

As Marcus walked out of the office, he saw the kid still standing at the file cabinet, pretending he hadn't heard everything. Then he pulled out his phone and dialed Karen.

"Are you okay?" she said when she answered.

Marcus stepped around Colby to his desk in the corner. "Yeah, I'm fine, but there's someone who isn't."

"Oh, and who is that?"

"You know the woman who was arrested at the scene, Reine Colbert?"

"Just from what Ryan told me."

"Well, she needs a lawyer, a good one. I need you to go over to County and be that for her."

Karen groaned on the other end and sighed. "This isn't going to be an easy case, is it?"

Marcus looked over his shoulder to Colby, who was now standing in the open office door, talking with Bert. Good, at least he wasn't listening. "No, but I need you to do what you can. Nothing about this is what it seems. Can you do that for me?"

He thought he heard tapping in the background, and he was pretty sure she'd dropped an f-bomb under her breath.

"Fine, but I swear, Marcus, you are really going to owe me big time for this."

"Thank you, Karen," he said, then hung up and took in his desk and the report he still needed to finish. He considered carefully the details he would need to include.

Chapter Fourteen

"You have no choice, Marcus. You're testifying," said Assistant DA Eileen Stanley. "I'm putting you on the stand, and the charges will go forward."

What was it with her? Eileen had dark hair and dark eyes, and her long nails were painted deep red against her dark skin. She was standing behind her desk, where she was preparing to throw the book at Reine Colbert.

To make it worse, Marcus hadn't heard back from Karen since the one text she had sent to tell him to stay far away from Reine after he'd shown up at the jail behind her to see what he could do to help. Apparently, because of his badge, he'd be forced to use everything Reine said against her. Maybe that was why he was standing before the assistant DA now, pleading for someone to see reason.

"Your charges are ridiculous," Marcus said. "As you saw in my report, she didn't understand what was happening. She was just trying to survive with her daughter the best she could. She knew nothing about Tommy Marshall, aiding and abetting, child endangerment, conspiring to aid and abet, hindering apprehension of a fugitive... Seriously,

Eileen? You know, what really pisses me off is this charge of obstruction of law enforcement engaged in official duty, which is a new low even for you."

It was on her face, in her expression. Evidently, she didn't like how he was speaking to her. She roughly tucked a file in her briefcase. The arraignment would be in just under an hour, and she wore a suit with a long skirt. It was Judge Thompson's court, and he insisted on formality from his lawyers: women in skirts, no pants, and men in a full suit and tie. Then there were his hair preferences: either short or tied back, with no long hair for men, and beards either freshly shaven or neatly trimmed.

"Look, there's no way you can prove she knew anything about an outstanding warrant on Tommy," Marcus said. "She had no idea he was a fugitive with a warrant out for attempted murder, and the circumstances of the charges against him were extenuating…"

She dragged her gaze up to him and held it, leaning on the desk on the palms of her hands. He knew she was working her way up to setting him straight. "Deputy O'Connell, I am well aware of your soft spot for the accused. It's been duly noted, but it is not up to me to prove or disprove the charges or clear the name of Tommy Marshall. He fled. There was an outstanding warrant. Reine Colbert was with him. Whether the sheriff decides to bring criminal charges is entirely up to him. You know this, Marcus."

She stood up and roughly gestured to him. "She was there in that house with him and was a party to the offense by aiding or assisting. Regardless of whether she did so before, during, or after the actual offense is completely irrelevant. The charges were filed, and I see no reason not to pursue them. If the judge decides to dismiss any of the charges, that is up to him, and the defense, I suspect, will likely have a bunch of motions to dismiss, but I guarantee you Judge Thompson is unlikely to do so. I've read both reports, yours and that of Deputy Lonnie Bush. Even if I were to choose not to pursue the matter of aiding and abetting, there is still the issue of her hindering the apprehension of a fugitive. Did you or did you not notify Tommy of his outstanding warrant in the presence of Reine Colbert?"

That was just something else that could add a nail to Reine's coffin. She would never again have her freedom. It wasn't looking good.

"As I thought," she stated before he could answer.

"You seem to forget she walked out of there with her daughter," Marcus said. "She didn't know any of this, and as soon as I was in there to clear it up and reason with Tommy to let her go, she was out the door. That isn't an accessory but a victim. A kidnapping, if you will. And child endangerment? Uh-uh, no way." He was shaking his head.

Eileen nodded, a tight smile on her lips. Just then, there was a knock on the open door, and he turned to see an older woman dressed much the same way Eileen was.

"Excuse me," she said. "You told me to remind you of the sentencing hearing for the Bower case at four?"

"Right, thank you, Susan," Eileen said, then inhaled. He could see she was hurried and not really in the mood to be reasonable when she turned her gaze back to him. "Look, Marcus, I understand you want some leniency here, but Montana laws are clear on child endangerment. If you hurt a child, you will be punished. In case you need a refresher, in the crime of child endangerment, the laws are broadly applied at the discretion of the DA and the sheriff. Considering an adult has a legal responsibility to make sure a child is free from unreasonably dangerous situations, when an adult screws up and fails to adequately protect her daughter, which is exactly what Reine Colbert did, it is called child endangerment.

"Let me clarify, if you're still unclear. Child endangerment occurs whenever a parent, guardian, or other adult caregiver allows a child to be placed or to remain in a dangerous, unhealthy, or inappropriate situation, whether intentionally or not. The beauty of this is that I don't even have to show that Reine Colbert intentionally meant to expose Eva to a dangerous situation. The courts are clear and apply a reasonable person standard in child endangerment cases. As you've said, Ms. Colbert didn't know, but that doesn't fly with the courts, because even if she didn't realize the situation was dangerous, reasonable people in that situation would have understood their actions could endanger the child's wellbeing.

"Being in a home with Tommy Marshall, who was both armed and dangerous… For that offense alone, she could get up to ten years, and with all the charges against her, I'm asking for a minimum of life unless your sister wants to talk a deal. At this point, though, I'm not too inclined to negotiate one, considering the strength of my case. It's a winner, and the final say is up to the judge in matters like this. You should know Judge Thompson is a stickler and is not known for leniency in these kinds of cases, and the DA has already made it clear that this is the kind of case that can go a long way to making the office look really good." She lifted her wrist, looked at her watch, and reached for her briefcase before striding around her desk to the door.

"What about the little girl, Eva?" Marcus said. He wondered if he'd ever get her image, her voice, out of his mind. She'd looked to him to help her, to save her, and where was she now? He didn't have a clue.

Eileen stopped in the doorway and turned to him, gripping her briefcase. "With child protective services, somewhere safe, and that's where she'll remain." It was so final, the way she said it. Then she added, "I expect you to be in court, Deputy, for the arraignment. I'll see you there."

Then she was out the door, and all Marcus could do was shake his head. There were times, and this was one of them, when he really hated the law and how it didn't always work. His cell phone rang as he took in the empty office, feeling tired, his stomach rumbling. He pulled it out and saw the number for the coroner's office.

"O'Connell," he said as he started out, seeing all the clerks, lawyers, and security on his way over to the courthouse across the street. Maybe he could catch Karen and find out if she would be able to work some miracle for Reine Colbert, considering the DA's office needed him to crucify a woman who just needed a fucking break.

"Deputy O'Connell, this is the coroner's office. I was told to let you know the next of kin for Tommy Marshall is here. We left a message for the sheriff, but your office said to call you."

He ran his hand through his hair and yanked, surprised as all hell. "Didn't expect his father to show. Guess everyone can have a change of heart…"

"It's not the father," the clerk said. "It's actually the deceased's mother and sister. They're here now. Did you want to stop by and speak with them?"

It took him a second to understand what he was saying. They were there now? He took in his watch, seeing court started in just under an hour. "You know what? I'm on my way. Will be there in five."

He'd made it to the county medical examiner's office in just under four minutes and parked out front, then pulled open the steel doors in the basement, feeling the eeriness of the place. Something about it had always bothered him.

He spotted the desk and two women, one young and blond, pretty, and one older, weeping. The resemblance was clear. He stopped at the desk, and the man in scrubs and a white coat behind it looked up.

"Deputy O'Connell," Marcus said. "Is this Tommy Marshall's next of kin?" He gestured to them, his voice low.

The clerk nodded. "Yes, that's the mother and sister. They just finished IDing the body. They're waiting for the coroner to sign off."

He only nodded, tapping the counter, and then stepped over to the two women. The younger one gave him all her attention. She was medium height, and it appeared she was expecting, with a small baby bump under her blue and white shirt.

"You're the family of Tommy Marshall?" he said. "I'm Deputy O'Connell, with the Livingston Police Department."

"I'm Samantha Lawson, Sam for short," the woman said. "I'm Tommy's sister. This is our mother, Helen."

Helen was teary eyed and said nothing. He couldn't imagine what she was going through, losing a son.

"I'm so sorry for your loss," he said. "This was a terrible tragedy."

Helen pulled a Kleenex from her pocket and wiped her eyes, her nose. Sam, though, seemed guarded as she nodded and said, "We haven't seen Tommy in years. We were told he refused to drop a gun, but it wasn't loaded. The coroner said he was shot several times, and one fatal shot to the chest killed him. I guess I don't understand why."

He could see her agony, which could likely turn to anger. "I guess he didn't see a way out. When was the last time either of you saw Tommy or spoke with him?" He wondered if they knew what had really happened, why Tommy had beaten the captain in the army.

"Not since he attacked that captain," Sam said. "He called me after and told me it wasn't what it seemed. I didn't know what he meant, but I begged him to turn himself in. At the same time, I knew he wouldn't. Dad wrote him off. He was furious with him for enlisting to begin with, for dropping out of college, for not becoming Thomas Marshall, Junior, and working under him in his company. At the time, I couldn't blame Tommy. He wasn't Dad. Right now, though, I wish he was. Maybe he'd still be here. You were in the cabin with him? That's our family's summer place. Haven't been there in years. Do you suppose we could go there, see it? Is there anything of Tommy's that we could have?"

As her daughter spoke, Helen seemed to pull herself together. The woman was in a fall coat and blue jeans, and when she looked up to him, he could see that she had the same eyes as Tommy.

"Yes, I was in the house," Marcus said. "I tried to talk him out of it. I'm sorry, though. The cabin is off limits. It's a crime scene. I know my office spoke with your husband, ma'am."

Helen shook her head. "Old fool! Unforgiving. He and Tommy never got along. You'd think they were polar opposites, only they were so much the same, with the same personality in some ways—strong minded, strong willed. Only Tommy was sensitive. My husband wouldn't even allow his name to be spoken, said he was a disgrace." She pulled in a breath, and he thought she was trying to hold it together.

The double doors opened to reveal the coroner, who walked over with a clipboard and papers. "We can release your son to you," he said, then began to lead

Helen out of the room. "You said you've made arrangements?"

Sam stayed where she was, arms crossed. Sadness seemed to ooze from her. "I heard what you tried to do for my brother, Deputy O'Connell. I spoke with the sheriff here, who said you did everything you could to reason with Tommy."

For a minute, he didn't know what to say, so he simply nodded. Finally, he said, "I wish I could have done more."

"We're having Tommy cremated here. Mom and I are going to the graveyard to decide on a headstone to memorialize him, but Mom wants to sprinkle his ashes at the cabin, so we may omit the stone. I'll leave it up to her. Tommy loved that place, so I can understand why he went there. At the same time, I know Dad will sell it now."

She said nothing else, and he glanced over to Helen, who was crying again as she strode back in with the coroner. Marcus pulled out his wallet and lifted out one of his cards, holding it out to Samantha.

"If you ever have any questions or just want to talk, there's my number," he said before he turned and left the coroner's office.

A family was grieving. A life had been lost.

He started over to the courthouse, knowing he couldn't do anything for Tommy, but Reine Colbert was still there, and so was her daughter, Eva. He could at least do what he could for them.

Chapter Fifteen

"Take the beer, Marcus," Suzanne said.

He was lounging in a patio chair on the front porch of Jenny and Ryan's. His brother had moved into the place, because Jenny wasn't about to move from a house she said was hers. What was it with women and houses?

Suzanne dangled the can in front of him, and he noted it was a pale ale rather than the dark ale only she drank. He popped the tab, and she took one of the five patio chairs lined up side by side on the porch beside him. Owen was out back, barbecuing, Jenny was in the kitchen with his mom, and Alison and Ryan were, he thought, watching the game in the living room. Karen still hadn't shown up, but then, he himself had arrived only five minutes ago, and after dutifully poking in his head to say hi, he had gone back outside. No one had said anything else.

"I need to leave in a minute," he said. "I'm only here following Mom's orders." He lifted the beer and took a swallow, feeling the weariness. He knew he should eat, but instead he leaned forward and dragged his hand over his face, hearing the scrape of whiskers.

"Yeah, well, we were worried. I can tell you Mom is breathing a sigh of relief inside. Ryan told me what happened to Reine Colbert's husband, a firefighter…"

He took in the modest homes on this street, a neighborhood of respectable families. He could actually picture Reine and her daughter and her husband having something just like this.

"It doesn't give you the warm and fuzzy American dream feeling, does it?" she said. "He's there to save everyone, but then the same system turns its back on him. You know, we don't talk about it at the station, but we all know we're at higher risk for cancer, with the kind of fires we walk into, the chemicals we breathe in, what we're exposed to. Then add in medical insurance…" She was shaking her head. "We've heard the stories. Some of the insurance companies are denying coverage based on obscure clauses that no average person can really understand. Of course, if you had unlimited resources, you could fight it and win, but after how many years, after you've lost everything? The sad thing, Marcus, is that what happened to Reine's husband, to Reine and Eva, could happen to anyone. No one is safe from that. It's terrifying, you know. They were fighting a giant who had everything on its side."

He took in the neighbors across the way, the early evening. The sun had dipped low on the horizon. He spotted Karen's practical four-door Honda pulling up in front, and when he heard the screen door behind him, he didn't have to look back to see that it was Ryan. He could hear the voices inside as they all watched Karen step out of her car. She was in a dark suit, skirt, and pumps, and her red hair was tied back in a ponytail, all a giveaway that she'd been in Thompson's court.

"So I heard they're talking about a deal for Reine," Ryan said. He was dressed in blue jeans and a faded blue shirt.

"She shouldn't have to settle," Suzanne replied.

Marcus didn't think he had anything left to say, considering he was of the mind that she'd gotten the short end of the stick. She hadn't been granted bail at the arraignment, not that she would've been able to afford it, anyways.

They all watched Karen start up the walk toward them, but she stopped at the bottom of the steps, giving them that look she had when a case didn't turn out the way she wanted. She just stared at each of them with those O'Connell blue eyes, then finally unbuttoned her blazer, revealing a white sleeveless blouse underneath. "Well, is there wine?" she said.

"Chilling in the fridge," Ryan said. "I'll grab you a glass."

Karen bent down and pulled off her pumps, standing barefoot now on the bottom step as she groaned. "Just bring the bottle, too. I may need more than one." She climbed up the steps and took the other chair on the porch, then reached over and rested her hand on Marcus's arm.

"How's Reine doing?" he said. He didn't look over to Karen, still taking in the neighborhood where his brother lived, the cars parked on the street, his cruiser parked in the driveway. What could his sister say? She was behind bars. It didn't get much worse.

"As good as can be expected. She took the deal. We'll be signing it in the morning. Don't beat yourself up, Marcus. You did all you could, and so did I. The law wasn't on her side in this one."

Not exactly the words of wisdom he wanted to hear. He lifted the beer and took another swallow, feeling the chill of the can and taking in the sounds of his family. "She was screwed over, Karen."

Ryan pushed open the screen and stepped out with a bottle of white wine and a glass filled halfway. He handed it to her, and she lifted her glass to him and took a big swallow. Ryan set the bottle on the porch by her bare feet.

"Ah, that's good," she said. "Thank you."

Ryan leaned again on the rail, and no one said anything for another minute.

"It could have been worse, Marcus," Karen said. "I got her sentence down to eight years. They wanted a ridiculous amount, thirty-five. She'll be out in three on good behavior. I'd consider that a win, given they also wanted to strip her rights as a parent. At least now she'll get a chance to see Eva."

"She shouldn't be in at all," he said, dragging his gaze over to his sister and seeing how frustrated she was, too.

"That's not the way it works. You know that. The jails are filled with people who shouldn't be there. I did what I could, but Eileen won't budge on this one, and neither will the DA. The judge is known for going hard on these kinds of crimes."

The chair creaked as Suzanne leaned forward around Marcus and really took in Karen. "So why is Eileen being such a hard-ass on this?"

Karen swirled her glass of wine and took another swallow. "All I know is these kinds of cases are personal to her. She's made it known that if the kinds of laws that are supposed to protect kids had been around when she was growing up, her sister would still be alive. She grew up in a house with her mother's boyfriend, and there were guns and bad people. Her sister got caught in the crossfire. She said a child should never have a gun shoved in her face.

The circumstances were different, but she won't see it any other way."

No one said anything else for a second.

"And Eva Colbert, what's going to happen to her?" Ryan asked. "Were you able to find out where she is?"

Marcus had already pulled up the name of the home where Eva had been placed, with other foster kids, under the care of an old woman. No one was ever there long. It was a bed, a roof, but not much else.

"I know where she is. I'll keep an eye out," Marcus said. It was all he could do in a system that had the worse record for turning out well-adjusted kids. He downed the rest of his beer and stood up, then handed the empty can to Ryan. His sisters were watching him, too. "Tell Mom I have to go, but I'll stop by tomorrow. And say goodbye to that niece of mine, Jenny, and Owen." He started down the steps, then turned back to his siblings. "Anyone hear from Luke when he's coming back?"

It had been nearly three months since their brother had shipped out. To where, exactly, none of them knew. They'd heard from him only once in the past month.

"No, it could be any day or several more weeks," Suzanne said. "Who knows what part of the world they've sent him and his team?"

Marcus simply nodded as he listened to the goodbyes and walked back to his cruiser. He climbed behind the wheel, seeing his cell phone and the fact that there were no messages. He needed sleep and food, as he thought of the omelette he hadn't finished that morning at his loft. Maybe he'd order some Chinese, considering he lived right above the takeout restaurant.

Then there was Charlotte. Normally, he never went this long in a day without talking to her.

He took in the town as he drove home, and the street

where he lived, and the Subaru that looked a lot like Charlotte's parked between a minivan and a pickup in front of the Chinese restaurant.

Marcus pulled into a reserved spot and stepped out of his cruiser and onto the sidewalk. Charlotte was standing by the door that led up to his loft. There was a duffle bag on the ground at her feet, and she was wearing a faded brown sweater and blue jeans. Her dark hair was hanging loose over her shoulders.

"You look tired, Marcus," she said as he stepped closer and stopping right in front of her.

"So what is this?" He gestured to her bag on the ground and the way she stood before him.

She lifted her ringless hand and pressed it over his chest. "Someone gave me some really good advice, and I figured it was time I listened." She didn't pull those hazel eyes from his. "I gave him the house."

For a minute, he didn't think he'd heard her right.

"But you love that house," Marcus said.

All she did was shake her head, and the way she was looking up at him held sorrow, passion, and so much more. "It's just four walls made of wood, Marcus. You told me that. A house can't make you happy, and I guess I finally realized that holding on to something, even though it was my grandparents' and had been in my family, wasn't going to bring me love. It's just a house, Marcus. I love you more."

He stepped closer, resting his hand over hers on his chest. Her other slid up and touched his cheek, running over the scab. "So you're just giving up, giving the house to Jimmy Roy?"

She pulled in a breath, licked her lips, and sighed. "No, I'm not giving up, Marcus. I'm choosing to move on. There's a difference. I spoke with Jimmy, told him he could have the house, but I was done fighting. I want the divorce now. I told him I was sorry and told him to take anything he wanted."

He took in the duffle bag at her feet. "So you're moving in?"

She slid her arms over his shoulders, and he settled his arms around her, feeling her heat against him. "I am, if that's all right?" she said softly.

"You know I don't care about a house, right? This is all I need, this place here," he said, wondering if she'd be okay in an old loft that was small and cramped.

She lifted her lips to meet him halfway, kissing him slow and easy. "Your place is cute, Marcus. As you've reminded me how many times, it's just four walls, and they won't bring you happiness. You, Marcus, you've always made me happy. That day so long ago when I was still with Jimmy and kissed you, do you remember what you said to me after he saw us, after you ate his fist?"

He just looked at her. He remembered well. He'd said he wasn't a homewrecker and would never be one. He slid his hand over her cheek, and she rested her hand over his.

"You were never a homewrecker, Marcus," she said. "I just never realized how much I really loved you. If I was honest then with myself, I'd have told you. You were never in the wrong. I was, for staying with him. I should have left Jimmy then."

He could see she wasn't going to pretend anymore that this, between them, wasn't real. He couldn't help himself from leaning down and kissing her again before pulling back, feeling an ease settle in after what had been a really crappy day.

"Well, then, let's get you moved in," he said, then reached for her duffle bag and unlocked the door that led up to his loft, gesturing for her to go first.

"Just one more thing, Marcus," Charlotte added. She turned and faced him again, touching him, running her hand over his chest, a touch that he knew he could get used to every day, every night. "When my divorce is final, I expect you'll ask me to marry you."

He took in the passion in her hazel eyes, the hint of a smile, before she turned and started up the stairs in front of him, and he just took in the curves of the woman he'd loved for a long time.

"Yes, and I won't wait a second longer, Charlotte," he said under his breath. Then he locked the door behind him and started up to his loft, behind the woman he'd started to believe could be his.

Chapter Sixteen

Sun spilled through the big window overlooking the street. The warm body in bed beside him was that of a woman he'd dreamed of being with for so long, but he'd never believed it would actually happen. Maybe that was why he'd forced the thought from his mind for too many years. Yet there she was now, on her side, softly snoring, a sound that he found mildly amusing.

He took a second as she slept to take in her round face, perfect lips, narrow nose, and thick dark lashes. She was closer to perfection to him than any woman he'd ever met. The sheet was twisted around her, and he could just make out her creamy white breasts peeking above it.

He should have felt at peace, considering the night she'd given him, the way she'd undressed him, kissing him, touching him tenderly in a way that surpassed his dreams. With each kiss, each touch, she had slid down on him while he rested his hands on her waist, her hips, the curves he'd always loved. He had guided her the entire time.

Yet here he was now, so unsettled.

He should have slept deeply, but the voice of that little

girl who had called to him to help her was still haunting him now. He ran his hand over his face, hearing the scrape of whiskers as he felt the knot again in his stomach, thinking of the ordeal the girl had been through. He'd seen worse, but it had been just one of those calls he never wanted to get.

Charlotte stirred and stretched against him with her softness and heat, and she blinked as a slow smile touched her lips. She reached over and touched him, his chest, his stomach, and lower. He hissed, and what did he do but rest his hand over hers to stop her? Was he out of his mind?

"What's wrong?" she asked as she pulled back and propped herself up on her elbow, looking down at him where he now lay on his back. Her gaze softened as she reached over and traced her fingers over his forehead, his hairline, through his thick dark hair, and he linked his fingers with hers.

"Eva was looking to me to save her," he said. "Now look at this mess. I even wrote in the report what she had said, that her mom was scared, they were both scared, but where is she now?"

He knew, though. She was in a foster home run by an old woman, a home he couldn't believe social services actually used.

"It's not your fault, Marcus," Charlotte said. "It's not up to you to fix everything for everyone, even though I know you feel responsible…"

That was exactly what he hadn't wanted to hear. He took in the furrow of her brows and grunted as he sat up, swinging his feet onto the cool wooden floor and seeing their clothes in a heap. Charlotte's duffle bag was still on the chair. She needed to unpack, and he'd have to make room in his drawers.

She slid her hand over his back, rubbing the ache in his

shoulder. She sighed behind him and pressed a kiss to the spot, then rested her chin on it as she slid her arms around him. "You can't let things go," she said. "I mean, what do you think you can do for her? You did it all, Marcus. It's just a shitty thing that happened." She kissed his shoulder again, her breasts pressing into his back.

He rested his hand on her arm and rubbed. "I should have pushed it harder, should have demanded the charges be dropped, for Bert to…"

"What, Marcus? In case you forgot, there's nothing you could do. I was there outside when you were still cuffed inside that house. Whatever Lonnie said, we all saw when Reine came out. Sheriff Frank made a decision, and whether you like it or not, whether the sheriff was in the right or not, he ordered that those charges be filed against her. It could've gone either way, but you know, pushing the way you did falls under insubordination. You could have been fired. You've been a cop long enough to know the one thing you never do is embarrass your fellow officers or the sheriff calling the shots, even if he's wrong. You won't win that."

It was sobering to realize how right she was. A cop could shoot a man in the back, kick down the door of the wrong house in a police raid and kill an entire family, or abuse a suspect in custody and he wouldn't get fired, but Marcus pushing the way he was to get Reine Colbert freed was a step too far. Sheriff Frank had filed charges, and so had Lonnie, and both were backed by Bert. To have them dropped would be making them admit they were wrong. Too many egos involved.

"Doesn't say much, does it, that it's easier to toss away a woman and her kid than admit to the public that we made a mistake? Wouldn't look good, you know."

Charlotte didn't say anything. This kind of thing never

had sat right with him. Maybe that was why he did what he did sometimes.

"They got a raw deal," he continued. "I saw how terrified Eva was in the house, her voice on the phone. I don't think I'll ever forget. She lost her father, and her world was ripped apart then, and now she's lost her mother, who was doing her best to survive in a system that took everything from them. Even her home and those basic things we have as kids—toys, a room, a bed, family photos, all gone. I don't know, Charlotte. I can't just let it sit as it is. It's not right. Maybe Frank and Lonnie and Bert can sleep at night knowing they've destroyed a life, but I sure can't."

He sighed again, and she just held on to him. Her touch should have helped, but he couldn't shake the image of Reine Colbert in court, in prison garb, handcuffed and being led away as if she were a common criminal. He was just glad Eva hadn't seen it. He knew his sister had done all she could, considering how screwed up this was.

"So what are you thinking of doing?" Charlotte said.

He slid around, settling his hand on her thigh as she curled her legs under her, sitting there naked on his bed with not even a hint of shyness. Her dark hair was a tousled mess, and damn, did she look downright sexy.

"I want to stop in and check on her, Eva—and Reine too, even though Karen told me to stay away."

Charlotte settled her hand on his thigh, touching him. There was something about her that calmed him as she lifted her gaze to him again. "I think that's a fine idea, Marcus," she said, and he leaned in and kissed her deeply, then pulled back just a bit. "But first, how about a shower? I'll make you some breakfast, and then..." She offered a teasing smile and dragged her gaze down, taking in all of him.

Yeah, he really could get used to this.

Chapter Seventeen

"You sure this is it?"

Marcus tapped on the door of a small older house just outside the downtown core, in a part of town that was both commercial and residential, between a house that had been busted for drugs just the year before and a two-story house with a pizza takeout restaurant on the main floor. Right, the perfect spot for druggies when they got the munchies and didn't want to walk too far.

He kept that thought to himself as he rested his foot on the single concrete stoop and knocked again on the screen door after figuring out the front bell was broken. "Yeah, unfortunately," he said. "I pulled up the address. She was sent here."

Behind him, Charlotte was dressed in her deputy shirt, her dark hair pulled back. His cruiser was parked out front, and he still had his sunglasses on. He heard footsteps over the squeak of the floor inside, and the inside door rattled as a woman pulled it open. She appeared to be in her seventies, short, a little on the plump side, with gray shoulder-length hair.

"Can I help you, officer?" she said, frowning, as she opened the screen door. She was in a bulky shirt and pants, and her other hand rested on a cane.

"Are you Rita Halloway?" he said.

She didn't smile as she nodded. "Yes, I am. What is this about?"

"I'm Deputy O'Connell. A little girl by the name of Eva Colbert was brought here last night."

"She's still sleeping, last I checked," Rita said. She pushed open the door, and Marcus took that as an invitation to step inside. Charlotte followed.

He heard a TV in the other room and pulled off his sunglasses tucking them in his shirtfront, and he took in the dated kitchen at the front of the house. It was clean, with a cast-iron fry pan on the small white stove and a glass of water on the counter.

"Ma, who's here?" said a tall lanky man with light hair and a beard, about his age. He wore jeans and a loose faded T-shirt. "Oh, the cops…"

Marcus didn't miss the alarm. That was just something that happened when he showed up, as if people expected him to know everything they were hiding.

"These deputies are from the sheriff's office," Rita said. "They're here about the little girl dropped off last night. Jay, can you check and see if she's awake yet?"

The man glanced over his shoulder to the hall and then started down it without saying anything.

"Is there a problem, Deputy?" Rita asked. Her voice was deep, husky.

Marcus stepped into the middle of the kitchen as Rita rested her hands on the counter. He knew Charlotte was right there. He found himself taking in the neat and tidy room. "No, I just wanted to check on Eva and see how she was doing. I was the deputy who took her call last night. It was a traumatic thing for her to go through. Is that your son?" He gestured with his chin.

Rita hobbled a few steps forward with her cane. "Yes, he's helping me out here."

Marcus hadn't remembered seeing the man's name on the list as part of the household, but then, social services didn't always seem to keep the most accurate records.

He heard voices and spotted Eva holding Jay's hand as she walked barefoot toward them, wearing an adult's T-shirt, her hair a mess, her eyes haunted. He walked over to her and squatted.

"Hey, Eva, remember me from last night? It's Deputy O'Connell. I wanted to come on by and check on you and see how you are."

Jay was still holding her hand, and she looked up to him and then over to Rita, the foster parent responsible for her. He wondered if she was looking to them for permission.

"Deputy O'Connell, where is my mommy? Is she with you?"

He lifted his gaze to Jay and looked pointedly at his hand, holding Eva's. Jay let it go and walked away, back into the dark living room, lit only by the flat-screen TV.

"Eva, I told you already, your mommy isn't coming," Rita said. "She's in jail. The police took her. She did a bad thing. That's why you're here. She won't be coming to get you."

Marcus dragged his gaze to the woman. In the living room, Jay was now sitting on the sofa in front of the TV. The news was on, and he didn't miss the fact that the sofa was covered in what looked like bedding, blankets and a pillow.

Eva's lip trembled. How could the woman be so cruel?

"Eva, I know this is a scary thing for you, but I

promised you I would see that you're safe," Marcus said. "Hey, come on, have a seat here at the table." He pulled out a chair and lifted her onto it, then pulled out another one. He wondered if she'd had anything to eat. "Are you hungry? Did you get anything last night? How about something now, breakfast?"

He didn't have a clue what else to say. He lifted his gaze over to Rita, who seemed to get it, as she reached into a cupboard and pulled out a bowl. Maybe she understood what was expected of her.

"I'm hungry," Eva said, and he didn't miss the tears in her eyes. "Can I see my mommy?"

"Hey, listen, I know you want to see your mommy," he said. "I'll tell you what. Let me see what I can do, but how about we get you some breakfast first? We'll see that you get everything you need."

Charlotte was watching Rita, who pulled out a box of cheap generic cereal and dumped some in a bowl, followed by skim milk from the fridge. So this was it? He pulled his gaze away, hearing Charlotte saying something about the milk, or maybe the cereal, or maybe something else entirely.

"You promise you'll take me to my mommy? I don't want to stay here," she said in almost a whisper. He knew well she didn't want the old woman to hear, and for a minute, he could see how scared she was, in a strange house with strangers. He couldn't imagine how he'd have felt if he were her. Rita put the bowl of cereal in front of her on the table. Cold and sterile—that was how this seemed to him.

"There's your breakfast, Eva. Come on, eat up," Rita said, then turned toward Marcus. "Don't start getting it in her head that she's seeing her mother, because I don't want to hear about it every hour, every day—and then the crying. Eva, at this point, you won't be seeing her. Deputy, you should know better." She walked away back into the kitchen. "Do you want some juice or something, too? Not sure if I have any. Considering the hour you showed up here, I wasn't prepared…"

Marcus took in the watery cereal. Not the best breakfast, and it wasn't lost on him how the woman sounded as if this were in some way Eva's fault.

"No juice," Rita said. "Looks like Jay drank the rest of it. I'll have to go to the store later and figure out something for dinner. Jay, I need you to head out to the store for some groceries!"

"Hey, Eva, slide around and eat," Marcus said, not liking how the old woman was talking.

Charlotte was standing in the kitchen, her arms crossed, looking around at everything. He knew by her expression that she wasn't impressed.

"I'm going to do everything I can, Eva," Marcus said. "This is just temporary, okay?"

Her eyes seemed hollow, filled with tears, and he rested his hand on her shoulder, feeling how small and thin she was.

"You remember Charlotte?" he said. "She was on the phone with you last night when you called in. Well, I brought her with me. That's her there."

Eva put the spoon down after taking a tiny bite. Her expression said enough about how bad it must have tasted. "She was really nice," she said, then turned her head. "She's pretty, too."

Marcus stood and gestured to Charlotte. "Charlotte, come on over and sit with Eva. I just want a word with Rita."

She must have understood, as she stepped in front of him, and he rested his hand on her shoulder, touching her as she sat and scooted her chair closer. She slid her arm around the little girl, comforting her. She just needed someone to give a damn.

He stepped into the kitchen, where Rita was leaning on her cane and extending a hard look his way.

"Deputy, when you come in here and give the girl all kinds of false promises, you're not helping her," she said. "She'll be whining and crying, and I can't have that. You think I'm not sympathetic? I am. I've been doing this a long time and have lost count of the number of kids dropped off here in the middle of the night because they were yanked from parents who couldn't look after them. I'm providing her a bed and three meals until something permanent can be found, but she needs to understand that she won't see her mother again unless the courts say she can. I've seen these kinds of things over and over with these kids. It's more than likely she'll never see her mother again. She'll be in and out of places, and then she'll be angry because she'll feel she's been abandoned—which she has. Let's be honest. I'm not getting too attached, because she'll be gone to some other place soon. Could be tomorrow, next week, next month, next year. Never know when. You understand there's no permanence here, so don't make it harder for her."

Marcus was standing in front of her, his back to Charlotte and Eva. He knew she couldn't hear, as Rita had thankfully kept her voice low. He was well aware of how this place wasn't the ideal spot for a little girl, and hearing just how bad it was made him sick to his stomach.

"Your son lives here?" He gestured with his chin, darting his head to see around the fridge and into the tiny living room.

"For now," Rita said. "Had to move him onto the sofa to give the bedroom to the girl."

He wanted to see the room, maybe to settle something in his mind, so he gestured to the hallway. "Down this way?"

She just nodded.

"How many kids are you fostering right now?" he said as he walked past the table, where Charlotte glanced up to him, her hand lingering over the back of Eva's chair. Something told him no one was doing what was best for this little girl.

"Right now, today?" Rita said. "Just her, but I can have two or three at any one time."

The house was small. He took in the bedrooms—three, he thought. The open door at the end of the hall revealed a double bed, an old dresser, and a guitar in a case in the corner. What looked like men's clothes were in the closet. He didn't miss the deadbolt on the door.

"This is where she stayed?" He took in the room and then the windows, which were locked.

"This is it," Rita said, looking down at the bed with its old quilt and pillow. "As I said, a bed. I'm right next door, and I'm a light sleeper, so I can hear her."

"You lock the door," he said.

Rita seemed to stand her ground. "At night? Yes. As I said, I'm a light sleeper, so I can hear her if she needs to go to the bathroom. I haven't lost one of these kids and am not about to start. You think I don't know that they don't want to be here? They never do, but they're in my care, and I'm not taking any chances with a runaway in the middle of the night. Now, if that's all, Deputy, I'd like to get her settled in."

Into what? he wondered as he started back down the hall to see that Jay had stepped out the back door, and cigarette smoke was coming in.

"Jay, move away from the house if you're out there,

smoking!" Rita called out. "Can't have that lingering back in here."

Marcus took in Charlotte and the plea on her face. She was sitting close to Eva, who had barely eaten anything of the watery cereal, which now looked like mush. He rested his hand on Eva's head, and she looked up to him.

"I'm going to go see your mommy," he said, "but I'm going to stop back in and see you later. You think you can be brave just a little bit longer?" He couldn't look at Charlotte, because he knew well she was ready to dig her heels in and not leave the girl there.

"You won't forget?" she said.

The last thing he wanted was to see the spark of life in her eyes diminish in any way.

"No way, not a chance," he said. Then he gestured to Charlotte as he started to the door, taking in the old woman talking to her son out back. Charlotte was leaning over Eva and brushing her hair from her face, then pressed a kiss to the top of her head—just something else he really loved about that woman.

Chapter Eighteen

"You can't leave her in that house, Marcus," Charlotte said for the fourth time as they drove to the office. "That's cruel and unusual punishment."

Even though he wanted to do something to get Eva out of that house, physically taking her was something he couldn't do, because social services were in charge. It would take a call and a whole lot of persuasion to do anything.

"You think I didn't want to pack her up and take her out of there?" he said. "Then what, Charlotte? You know it doesn't work that way."

"They're not fit to look after a child," she said, sitting stubbornly in the passenger side. Of course, she was upset. So was he.

"It's passable, and there're worse places," he said. "I'll make a call to the social worker and find out what's what."

He knew she was giving him everything as he pulled up and parked beside the sheriff's car. So he was in the office that morning. Good.

"You do more than that, Marcus," she said. "She can't spend another night there."

He let out a sigh as he turned off the cruiser and just stared up at the building, seeing Colby, the kid, walk in ahead of them. He didn't answer, though, as he pulled his hand over his face. He really did need to shave, but it seemed there were just more important things right now.

"There may not be anywhere else for her," he said. "If they were living on the streets, I would think no close family could take her. I'm sure they're looking."

Then there was Reine, who was in jail now. He really needed to talk to her.

He dragged his gaze over to Charlotte and opened his door. At the same time, she opened hers and stepped out. The sun was bright; the day was warm. He walked around and met her halfway, stopping on the sidewalk in front of the cruiser. She tapped his arm, and he pulled her closer, her hands settling over his duty belt, around his waist. She let out a sigh.

"I can see you're upset," he said. "It's not sitting right with me, either. Go on. You need to get into work and man the phones."

She nodded, but she didn't step away.

"I'll figure something out," he continued. "I'll find another option for her."

This time, she did step back, and the look she gave him was that stubborn look he'd seen too many times. "And what option would that be? You think I don't know that her being where she is means they couldn't really find a place for her? I know how flawed it is. Too many kids need a place, and there aren't enough good ones for them." She paused. "Let's take her."

He wasn't sure he'd heard her right. He lifted his gaze to the sheriff's office, knowing he needed to make his presence known, but that would be after he saw Reine. "Take her where, exactly, Charlotte? I have a bachelor pad that's barely big enough for the two of us, nowhere to put your stuff. Where would we put her? Even if I wanted to, I don't know how it could work." He was shaking his head, but Charlotte didn't pull her gaze from him and seemed to dig in further.

"Then we'll get a bigger place," she said. "We'll make do until we do. Don't make it difficult, Marcus. I saw the way you looked at her. You care."

What kind of statement was that? "Of course I care. I'm not a monster. Anyone with a beating heart would care, but how would us taking her make it any better for her?"

He didn't need her to answer that, though. He knew it would.

"It would make a difference, Marcus, but I think you already know that. We could make it work."

It was the way she said it. He leaned down and pressed a kiss to her lips, letting it linger, before he pulled back and spotted Lonnie stepping out of the station, hesitating, watching them. Then he was coming their way.

Of course, Charlotte sensed the anger he was now feeling, which he couldn't hide, not from her. "You go see Reine," she said, "but call the social worker, too. See if you can work something out." Then she ran her hand over his chest and stepped away just as Lonnie approached. "Hey there, Lonnie," was all she said as she lifted her hand in a wave and strode away up the steps.

"So, you and Charlotte…" Lonnie started.

Marcus gave him everything in that moment. He wondered if he had any idea right now how much he would rather be talking to anyone else. "Where're you off to?" he finally said, crossing his arms, wondering what it was about Lonnie that seemed rattled, off.

"On a call," he said. "Another vandalism. Kids, they think. Nuisance, really. Look, I'm sorry for how everything went down. The sheriff is doing well today." He gestured behind him.

Marcus was glad for that much. Maybe Bert had realized how much he was needed. He said nothing.

"Listen, Marcus, I don't want this to be a thing," he said. "I heard that Ms. Colbert took a deal."

There it was, exactly what he didn't want to talk about with him.

"Still shouldn't have happened, Lonnie," he said. "She didn't get a fair shake. I was in the house, not you. You were wrong, what you did. Sheriff Frank was, too, and Bert. Still can't believe he let it stand."

Lonnie reached over and rested his hand on Marcus's shoulder, and of course his gaze went right there. He pulled his hand away and stepped back. "It's not on you, Marcus. The law isn't always fair. Bert said he was stepping down, and you'll be taking his place as sheriff."

So maybe that was it. Lonnie wanted to make sure there was still a place for him. Marcus just dragged his gaze up to the office and then back to his fellow officer.

"You run into any problems, you let me know out there," he said. It was all he could make himself say. He walked back to his cruiser and climbed behind the wheel.

After a short drive, he parked behind the jail, a place he'd been too many times, dragging people he'd arrested and having them booked. But this time he felt as if he were seeing everything through different eyes. It was concrete, loud.

Getting in to see Reine Colbert was easy, considering he was the deputy in charge. He was waiting in a room when she was led in, wearing cuffs and an orange baggy jumpsuit that seemed to hang off her frame. He wasn't sure what to make of the way she was looking at him.

"You can take off the cuffs," he said to the female guard.

Reine acknowledged him with a nod, then rubbed her wrists, which had him remembering the bite of cuffs on his own wrists. "Your sister said I wasn't supposed to talk to you."

Of course she had. Karen was good.

"Since you made a deal, Reine, it's kind of a moot point now," he said, then gestured to one of the steel chairs by the table, where he knew lawyer after lawyer had sat with their clients. The walls were gray. The place was depressing. "Wanted to check on you and see how you're doing. I stopped in to see Eva this morning."

She slid into one of the chairs, but she couldn't hide the tear that spilled out. "How is she?" She sounded desperate. How could she not? She wasn't a mother who didn't care.

"She's good," he said. Of course, she wasn't, but telling her mother what he'd seen would only drive her crazy in a place where she could do nothing for her daughter. "Do you have any family, Reine? Anyone who could take Eva while you're doing your time?"

She said nothing for a second as she pulled her lower lip between her teeth and shook her head. "No one who could do anything. I'm estranged from my father. I have an aunt in Glasgow, Scotland, who I met twice when I was a kid. My husband's mother is down in New Mexico, but she suffers from bipolar. His brother is a used car salesman in Spokane, last we heard. They were never close. I met his mom. She's good if she's on her meds, a disaster if she's not. My husband never wanted her in Eva's life." She made a face and clasped her hands, resting them on the steel table. "Your sister asked me to reach out to my father, at least for Eva."

He waited for more. Maybe she was still considering, from the way she looked away and wiped the tear from her face. He pulled out the chair across from her and sat down, and she forced a smile to her face, but he suspected it was because she didn't know what else to do.

"You should, unless there's a reason he shouldn't know about Eva?" he said.

She was shaking her head. "He's not a bad man in that way, so to speak. We're just estranged. He never liked Vern, my husband, but how many fathers really like the men involved with their daughters? He told me to end it, I said no, and he said Vern would never amount to anything. I said he was wrong. My husband was a hero, a good man. My father never showed up for my wedding. That said everything."

So it was anger. Marcus wondered if the man would show up now, considering where his daughter was.

"Karen said the DA wants to strip me of my parental rights," Reine said. "I said no, and the only reason I took the deal offered was because I can't gamble on never seeing my daughter again. I could be out in three years, your sister said. Eva will be nine. I can live with that. Life without her? I can't."

He wondered if she understood what three years in the system would do to a kid. "I'm sorry it went down this way," he said. "You don't deserve this."

"So are you lying to me, Deputy O'Connell, about my daughter? I don't know how she could be okay after what happened. I didn't know anything about Tommy, but he was the only one who tried to help us. You know, he brought food for people in the camp who were hungry. He wasn't a bad man. I didn't realize until later that he was haunted by his time in the military. There was just a look in his eyes: One minute he was there, and the next he wasn't. He never meant to scare us."

"I know that," he said, taking Reine in. He knew Tommy would never have shared what really had happened, what had made him snap and attack his captain. He couldn't help wondering now why Tommy had shared that haunting story with him.

"You were nice to us, Deputy," Reine said. "The way you tried to reason with Tommy, you're a good man. You remind me so much of Vern. You're a lot like him."

"I want to take Eva while you're here," he said suddenly. "She should be with people who care. My girlfriend, Charlotte, and I would like to take her. I wanted to talk to you about it."

She shut her eyes for a second and then looked over to him. "You would look out for her, wouldn't you?" she said. From the way she asked, he knew she just wanted someone to do something.

He nodded. "With everything I have. You have my word. Charlotte and I will make sure she's looked after and loved."

She sniffed and wiped at more tears that continued to fall. "If I could go back, I wouldn't have cuffed you to that chair," she said. "I didn't know…" Then she nodded. "Yes, I think you would look after her. Would you bring her to see me?"

He just looked over to the woman he wished his sister could have done more for. "Of course we will," he said. "You're still her mother."

Chapter Nineteen

"Don't think I've seen Mom so happy," said Suzanne. "First Ryan and the surprise teenage granddaughter, Alison, and now you with Eva." She held out a beer to him, a light lager, where he lingered in his mom's backyard.

Owen was flipping burgers, appearing unusually quiet. His mom, whom he could see through the open back door, was in the kitchen with Karen, Charlotte, Alison, Jenny, and Eva, who was perched on a stool at the island, tucked between Charlotte and Alison and being fussed over by everyone.

"You know that little girl has stolen everyone's hearts," Suzanne said.

What could he say? From the moment he'd picked her up from Rita's house, he'd breathed out a sigh of relief for the first time since this shitstorm had started. "I know," he said. "I see Mom is spoiling her in there."

"Mom expects to look after her when you and Charlotte are working. Heard you're taking her to see her mom at the prison this weekend, too. You think it's okay, taking her into a place a kid shouldn't be?"

He didn't miss the overprotectiveness in her tone. As soon as his family had learned about Eva and realized she was now a part of their family, they had circled the wagons around her. How could he explain that he'd promised Reine, and he knew how much Eva needed to see her?

Owen tossed him a look over his shoulder, clearly having listened in. "Suzanne's right. You may do more harm than good, Marcus. She's only six."

He'd never heard his brother talk like that. "It's worse if she doesn't see her. She'll be fine. I'll see to it, and so will Charlotte."

Ryan stepped out of the house in his park uniform, taking them in. "Mom said to throw on another hot dog for Eva in case she wants two," he said.

Marcus just took in his brother, who hadn't really said anything to him since he'd told him that Reine had signed over temporary guardianship to him and Charlotte while she served her time. Karen had been furious that he'd talked with Reine behind her back, but she'd honored her wishes and agreed that Charlotte and Marcus would be a better solution to looking after Eva. She'd handled the agreement, getting it signed before a judge, and Marcus and Charlotte had picked her up before she had to spend one more night under a roof with a woman who wouldn't let herself care too much.

"So did you smooth things over with Karen yet?" Ryan asked. Suzanne made a face, and Owen added another dog to the barbecue and pretended not to listen.

"I plan to tonight," Marcus said, knowing that Karen wouldn't make it easy, which was why he was out back and she was inside the kitchen. He could hear the laughter, and he knew he couldn't wait any longer. "Well, can't put it off. Wish me luck." He took a swallow of beer and started to the house, feeling Ryan pat his shoulder as he passed.

When he stepped into the kitchen, six pairs of eyes landed on him, and everyone went quiet.

"So this is where the fun is," he said. He took in Eva, who was still perched on a stool between Alison, who had appointed herself her official big sister, and Charlotte, who he knew had fallen in love with her the first night they'd brought her home.

"Is Owen almost finished out there? The kids are getting hungry," his mom said.

Meanwhile, Karen gave everything to the glass of wine she was holding. Just that stubborn O'Connell streak. She was refusing to make this easy on him.

"Shouldn't be much longer," he said.

His mom started to the back door with an empty platter. She was in blue jeans and a floral peasant shirt, with tiny pearls in her ears, her hair short and stylish. She stopped beside him and set her hand on his arm, looking up at him with that motherly look she adopted when she had something on her mind. "You did a good thing, getting that girl. She's now a part of our family. You know that, though. You and Charlotte are working tomorrow, so I'm taking both my granddaughters shopping—and I plan to spoil Eva, just so you know. You did all you could, so give yourself a break, and go make it right with your sister."

As his mom stepped outside, he took in how Charlotte and Jenny were leaned against the island, wine in hand, talking, both very aware of the showdown that was likely to happen.

"Karen, can I have a word?" he said, and what did his sister do but drag her gaze over and then start into the living room? No one said anything. Both Charlotte and Jenny gave him a look of sympathy.

He stepped around the island and rested his hand on Alison's brown hair, which was still growing out, and then on Eva's. Then he settled his hand on Eva's shoulder when she smiled up at him. "Hot dogs are almost ready," he said. "Your grandma's getting some for you."

He knew it was the first time he'd said it, even though his mom had insisted from day one that Eva call her Grandma. Then he walked into the living room, where his brooding sister was lounging in the spot where his brother Luke always sat when he was home on leave.

He forced himself to sit on the stool across from her, then really looked at the living room. It had changed some over the years, but it was still the same. "You going to continue giving me the silent treatment?" he finally said.

Karen lifted those O'Connell blue eyes to him, and they really packed a punch. "Is that your way of apologizing, Marcus? Because if it is, it sucks big time." She was direct and to the point.

"If you want me to say I'm sorry for seeing your client without talking to you first, I'll say I'm sorry—but I'm not, because maybe things wouldn't have turned out this way otherwise. You know Charlotte had to hold Eva until she fell asleep the first two nights? She woke up twice, crying, nightmares."

For now, Eva was sleeping on a cot only five feet from Charlotte's side of the bed in their one-room bachelor pad.

Karen said nothing, but he didn't miss the way she flinched. "I didn't know," she said. "Heard you're looking for a bigger place."

Actually, he'd found one already, a small house, two bedrooms, a block from his mom's house. He just hadn't told everyone yet. He'd signed the lease papers with Charlotte that morning, and they were taking possession on the first of the coming month.

"A bachelor pad doesn't work with an instant family," he said. "We're crammed in like sardines, and Charlotte and I kind of need our own bedroom with a door. You know, can't remember the last time I slept in pajamas. Never owned a pair, so there I was in the store, having to buy some."

His sister couldn't help smiling. Then she turned serious. "I like Charlotte, always have. I think she's good for you. Heard Jimmy signed the divorce papers."

He grunted. "She let him have the house. Left him with nothing else to argue about, so he had no reason to keep on fighting."

Karen swirled her wine and was staring across the table at him. He knew she had something else on her mind. "I heard back from Reine's father," she said. "I reached out to him for Reine. He's going to see her. Sounds like he's going to bring in his own lawyer and try to appeal. You should know he said he wants to see Eva."

The knot that had eased only a few days ago returned. He could lose her. He dragged his gaze back to the kitchen, seeing how Eva was tucked close to Charlotte and how much she loved her already.

"But he's not planning on seeking custody," Karen said. "He's remarried and travels. He said as long as Eva is happy and taken care of..."

He pulled his gaze back to his sister. "So he won't be stepping in and taking her?"

She just shook her head. "No. He spoke with Reine and said he'd respect her wishes. Seems she said you and Charlotte taking Eva will make her time easier. She could see how much you cared and that Eva will be okay, that you'll make sure of it. I told her we're a big family, and we'll all make sure she's okay and looked after. Seemed to be what she needed to hear."

He just nodded and dangled his beer, feeling as if there was more.

"Heard Bert stepped down, too," Karen said. "Next week, you're officially the new sheriff until the next election."

Then there was that.

"Just came a little too late," he said. "If only…"

Karen pulled in a breath. "Well, Marcus, if anything good will come out of this, at least you'll run things differently. The kindness you showed Reine… Marcus, you've always treated everyone with the same respect and dignity you would want to be treated with in the same circumstances. I remember you saying that once, but seeing it now, you really are going to make a difference here."

From the backyard, Owen called out, "Burgers are ready! Come and dish up."

Karen stood up and rested her hand on his shoulder as she went to walk past. "Heard too that you've been ordered by the city council to hire a woman for the new deputy position."

Right. There was that as well, the political side of things. He groaned as he thought of the resumes he'd been provided by the mayor. "Yeah," was all he said.

Karen smiled down on him. "Well, if anyone can handle the task, I'm sure you'll do just fine," she said.

He followed her into the kitchen, seeing Alison helping Eva dress a dog with a bottle of mustard, and he took in the woman he loved as she strode over to him and slid her arm around his waist.

"So, everything good?" she said.

He knew what she was asking, and he looked over to Karen, who was laughing over something Suzanne had said. The only one missing was Luke. He just hoped that tomorrow, they'd hear when he'd finally be coming home.

"Yeah, everything's perfect," he said, then leaned down and kissed Charlotte. He was no longer single but a man with an instant family. It really didn't get any better than this.

Turn the page for a sneak peek of
*THE SECRET HUSBAND the next book in THE
O'CONNELLS*
Available in print, eBook & audio

The Secret Husband

THE O'CONNELLS

Small-town lawyer Karen O'Connell believes that all of her clients who have found themselves recklessly embroiled in scandal and trouble have done so foolishly because of love. She has heard far too many times that the heart wants what it wants.

But one night, Karen receives a call from Jack Curtis, her vengeful ex-husband, whom she's never told anyone in her family about. He's found himself in a world of trouble, arrested and in jail, charged with murder.

He says he's innocent, and he needs her help.

Her first response is to say no, but Karen knows Jack isn't the kind of guy to ask for help from anyone, especially not from the ex-wife he openly despises and hasn't seen in years. She knows there must be more to the story—but what she doesn't know is that the mysterious circumstances surrounding the murder could be the reason her hasty marriage ended so badly.

The Secret Husband - Chapter 1

Although some couples bragged of Friday date nights filled with romance and dinner, followed by extremely hot sex, Karen O'Connell's Friday nights unfortunately consisted of a quiet, darkened office, a shot of whiskey, and the locked drawer in her desk that only she ever went into.

She stared at the names on the files that filled the drawer, names that were meaningless to the masses but left her reaching for the bottle of whiskey she kept tucked in the back, a single short lead-cut crystal highball glass, and a green velvet ring box. The drawer was a constant reminder, like an albatross around her neck, of everything wrong with her life.

At the same time, she only ever opened it on Friday nights or whenever she needed to add yet another file from a case where she hadn't gotten the win her client deserved. It was a drawer that, she supposed, if she had to put a label on it, symbolized sorrow, heartache, pain, grief, anger, every sickening emotion that seemed to encompass what the legal system was becoming more and more as of late.

These were the kinds of defeat and sorrow she didn't share with anyone. How could she? Right and wrong seemed so unfair, leaving her filled with such anger, a trait in her that others considered unreasonable. At times, people compared her to a pit bull, not understanding what really drove her. But considering the names on these files all came with faces that haunted Karen every night when she closed her eyes, this was a fight she couldn't figure out how to win.

Why did she do this to herself? If she were like every other lawyer out there, she'd have told herself she'd done the best she could, that this was just the nature of her job, and to move on. But to Karen, these lost cases were lives that had been destroyed—mothers, daughters, fathers, brothers, husbands. They were each someone's child, and every one of them had been on the wrong side of the crapshoot called justice. Being on the other side left Karen feeling so damn helpless.

She lifted the short glass and downed another swallow of the two fingers of whiskey, her secret indulgence, one no one in her family knew about. She kicked off her pumps, letting her bare toes dig into the carpet, and swiveled around and leaned back in her chair, taking in the two large windows that looked out at the darkened downtown.

Just then, the phone started ringing, and she did what she always did on Friday night: ignored it and let voicemail pick it up.

She waited until it stopped ringing before she settled into the vibration of the bass from the downstairs bar, welcoming the distraction. In that second of near silence, she lifted the glass and took a swallow, relishing the burn and then letting out a sigh. She turned back around, taking in the pile of files and seeing Reine Colbert's on top, her most recent case. As she opened the file and took in everything, the angst of it had her wishing she could have done more for a woman she felt had been screwed by everyone. She lifted the bottle, seeing it was half full, and poured another two fingers just as her cell phone lit up.

"Persistent, aren't they?" she said to no one as she took in the caller ID. It was Owen, her brother, who'd been more of a father to her—to all of the siblings, even though he'd been just a kid himself—than their own dad, whom she'd loved more than anything but who had decided to fuck off one day without even a goodbye to any of them.

Her hand hovered over the red decline, but at the same time, Owen was the one who never called. She answered. "Any chance that was you who called the office a second ago?"

"So you are there," he said. "Is that how you answer the phone?"

She didn't pick up her cell phone but left it on the desk, leaving the speaker on. Her brother's voice seemed to hold an edge. "It is when someone's phoning and bugging me when I just want to be left alone." She swirled the amber liquid, welcoming the burn as she made herself close up Reine's file. Under it was Lawrence Green's, another sad case, one of her first where the defendant ended up doing time for a crime she knew, deep down, he hadn't committed.

"I guess that answers my question as to where you are. Was just at Marcus and Charlotte's new place, setting up Eva's bunk bed. We just picked it up. Everyone's there except you. Suzanne said you've got some standing appointment on Fridays, and Ryan said he'd heard that too, but then, as everyone was talking about you, which you know we all do, things just didn't jive. I know you stay at the office every Friday night, but doing what? That, I haven't figured out yet."

She couldn't help the amusement that tugged at her lips even though she felt like crap, considering Owen was a plumber, not a detective. "You spying on me?"

He said nothing for a second, and she wasn't sure what she heard in the background. "Don't need to. Generally, I just know what you're doing, what you're thinking, where you are, and when something is off with you. The fact that your office light is still on…"

She turned in her chair, feeling the hair on the back of her neck spike. "Uh…where are you?" She stood up, going to the window and looking out and down on the street, where her brother's plumbing van was parked out front.

Owen was standing there on the sidewalk, looking up and giving her a wave. "Let me in," he said. "Your door's locked." Then he hung up.

"Shit…" she said under her breath.

There was something about him tonight. On the phone, Owen hadn't sounded like himself. She wasn't in the mood to talk, but she rested the glass on the desk with the files and hurried barefoot to her office door. After pulling it open, she took in the empty desk of the receptionist she still needed to hire and strode to the stairs, down the dirty wood steps, which needed a sweep and a wash.

Her brother was looking at her through the commercial glass. She'd see what he wanted and send him on his way. Owen was dressed as he always was, blue jeans that had seen better days and a T-shirt, always appearing as if he'd just been at a jobsite. She, meanwhile, was still in her navy dress.

She flicked the lock, and he pulled the door open and somehow maneuvered her back as he stepped in, flicking the deadbolt behind him. He was the same height and build as all her brothers, tall and broad shouldered, and he had the same O'Connell blue eyes as all of them, but at least he'd shaved.

"Drinking alone?" Ah, so he could smell it.

"And working…" she started as she crossed her arms, taking in the way he looked down at her before starting up the stairs ahead of her. "Where are you going?"

"Upstairs, to your office," he said, and she hurried after him, wanting to stuff the files back in the drawer along with the whiskey, which was sitting open on her desk.

"Hey, Owen, just give me a second to clean up…" she said as she raced around him to her door, not having to turn around to know he was right behind her.

"You have a new client or case coming up?"

She reached for the bottle and screwed the cap back on, not missing his expression, the way he was taking in her desk, the files, the bottle, everything.

"Wow, single malt, strong, bold. You can pour me a glass," he said, not waiting for her answer.

Her brain was still trying to come up with a story that sounded reasonable as she watched her brother make himself comfortable in the chair across her desk, where every client who came to her for help sat. Owen, though, lifted his sneakered feet and rested them on her desk, crossing them. His gaze took in the files again, and she couldn't help feeling as if he were seeing into her secret, private self, which she showed no one.

She just held the bottle and took in the glass on her desk, then the washed empty mug that had held her coffee that morning. She poured a splash in the mug and took in his gesture for more.

"Bad day?" he added as she handed him the mug before sitting down in her chair and lifting her own glass.

She considered what to say, resting her hand on the

files as Owen's gaze locked on to hers. Of course, he could see the names. She had a thing for big bold print on file tabs.

"Same as any other," she finally replied and settled her glass back on the desk. She gathered the files and stuffed them back into the drawer along with the bottle of whiskey, then closed it and turned the key, which was still in the lock. She pulled it out and rested it on the desk, taking in the way her brother was watching her.

"You know you did the best you could," he said. "No one could have done more than you. Give yourself a break. So is this you punishing yourself? I don't get it."

She didn't say anything for a second, then took in the smile that really wasn't a smile on her brother's face as he lifted the mug and downed the rest of the liquor. The way he pulled in a breath, she knew he too relished the burn.

She went to say something, then decided against it, lifting her glass and swirling around the amber liquid. "So what are you doing here?"

Owen rested the mug on her old scratched desk and took his time looking around her office. "Truth? Checking on you, considering what happened to Reine Colbert. I knew you took it hard, and everyone was wondering about you and how you really are. This looks like a Friday night pity party."

She froze, listening to the tick of the clock on the wall above the file cabinet, which held cases and clients and documents that didn't carry the same emotional baggage that her drawer of sorrow did. She flicked her gaze up and took in the intensity of her brother's gaze. Okay, so he knew, maybe?

"Ah…" was all she could get out. She sat back in her chair, hearing the woosh. "Pity party." She tried to conjure up something profound, but nothing came.

Owen just lifted his hand and waved, that same motion he had used with all of them, growing up, when he wanted them to stop whatever bullshit was about to come out of their mouths. How in the hell had he ever managed to step into the role of their father? He'd been just a teenager, sixteen.

"You think I didn't figure it out some time ago?" he said. "This Friday night thing, this ritual you have…" He gestured to her desk, her glass. "Drinking whiskey and staying at the office—doing what, I wasn't really sure. I have to wonder, from those old case files on your desk, if that's part of it."

"What do you think you know? Seriously, Owen, every good lawyer looks at those lost cases because that's what makes you get better. You're being ridiculous. So what if I'm here, working?" Her bare feet hit the floor, and both her palms were flat on the desk.

Owen jabbed a finger to her glass. "You're drinking the hard stuff that you never drink."

"Who else knows?"

He raised a brow, always the silent observer. "Well, I had an idea. Pretty sure Luke does too. I know Suzanne has wondered. Marcus and Ryan…" He just shrugged. "They're wrapped up in their stuff. Every Friday night you make some excuse, yet I see the lights on in your office, and I figured out the whiskey thing because Marcus mentioned he spotted you leaving the liquor store with it. Suzanne said she's seen you leaving the office late on Friday night a couple times when she's been out on a call, and you walk instead of drive. We all know when you've been drinking. Luke said we need to give you space while you figure out how to deal with a bad loss, because we know how personally you take your cases. You seem to forget I listen to everyone and put the puzzle together.

Guess I just don't understand why you put yourself through it."

There it was. Her secret was unraveling. How could she explain to anyone when she didn't understand herself?

"Is it too much for a little privacy in this family?" she said, reaching for her glass and leaning back. She turned her chair to the side as she took another swallow.

"Karen, Karen, Karen, you should know better. Privacy in our family? You forget, I've been watching your back for how long? As for the whiskey thing, don't worry. No one in the family would believe you drink it. Marcus likely thought you were picking it up for someone. This pity party, you looking at those cases or whatever you're doing, no one else has figured it out."

"But you have." She turned to her brother, who ran his hand over his face.

He was handsome, a catch, yet he was as single as she, Luke and Suzanne were. The one that they all depended on, Owen was only a few years older than they were, yet he had been a father to them all. Maybe the day their father left was the day she'd decided to hide everything she was thinking and feeling. Every man who'd ever said he loved her had turned his back on her and walked away, except her brothers.

"Yeah, always had my eye on you," Owen said. "The trouble you'd get into… Your prickly personality pushes everyone away, and at times you just can't help but make things difficult for yourself, with the way you'd scrap with Mom, with anyone and everyone. You need to let those cases go. You did more than anyone could do."

"They got a raw deal, Owen. You know, when I went to law school and then started practicing, I never realized law is just a different version of poker, a game of chance, where your life is in the hands of someone who doesn't know who you truly are. It's a toss of the dice, all up to whether the DA got laid the night before, or is fighting with his wife, or has profiled you because of the color of your skin, or because you're poor, or because you're a woman, or because you didn't come from a good home, a good neighborhood, or because you pissed off the wrong person, because, because... I could keep going. Racial and social profiling are things everyone does, but at the same time, you'll never get a judge, DA, or defense lawyer, never mind your average person out there, to admit they do it, because then they'd have to admit that this broken system doesn't work, and everyone's preconceived ideas about people and situations are in fact what should be on trial."

There she went, on a roll. She wasn't sure, by the way her brother cocked a brow, whether he was about to mock her, scold her, or tell her to get over herself.

Instead, he pulled in a breath. "Wow, you really are stuck in a dark place. I hope this isn't a place you go often, as it's not helping you or anyone and can make you bitter."

The way he said it felt so much like a scolding that she wanted to snarl.

He held up a hand. "You think I don't know all that? Of course I do. I saw the closed doors Mom faced, even though no one else did. But give yourself a break, Karen. It's the way the world works and always has. You're making a difference, and you need to start looking at what's working instead of what isn't. This dark place your head is in isn't doing you any good."

He gestured to her desk. "I know all those cases you've lost stick with you. If you had been any other lawyer, though, it would have been far worse for them. Reine Colbert would have gotten a lot more time, Lawrence Green would've been in a supermax in another state, where his family couldn't visit, Janine Baker wouldn't be up for parole next month, with a chance to reunite with her family, and Matt Wilky would never see the light of day again instead of having the chance of parole in fifteen years, all because he was in the wrong place at the wrong time.

"You want me to go on? Yeah, those cases sucked, and I saw how you took what happened personally after each one. But no one could have done better. It was a crapshoot for them anyway. You think I don't know how you see a part of yourself in those cases that everyone else calls a lost cause? So how about you start telling yourself that you give a damn, and you did what you could, but it's not all on you?"

She just stared at her brother. "Is this a pep talk?" She settled her glass on the desk, crossing her legs again, leaning back. "Because, in case you didn't get the memo, I'm a big girl and can look after myself."

"If that's what you need to tell yourself, then so be it, but you're still my little sister, and a pain in the ass, too. You always did take things way too personally. You can't fix everything for everyone. Sometimes you're just going to have to tell yourself that you did all you could, and that's the best that can be hoped for. Life isn't always fair, Karen. It can suck sometimes, too."

She didn't know why, but the way Owen said it had her leaning forward on the desk, really looking at him. He never said anything about what was going on in his life. Instead, he was always steady for all of them.

"You okay there, Owen? You know, I'm getting the feeling something is going on with you. You know you don't always have to be the one who carries everything for everyone else. You know you can tell me—" she started just as the office phone rang. She stared at it, and so did her brother. Damn the interruption. Who the hell was calling now?

"You going to answer that?" he said.

Well, Owen showing up here had ruined her melancholic Friday night alone time anyway. She hadn't even had the chance to settle into the files, which were back under lock and key. She let out a sigh and reached for the phone.

"So who is it?" Owen said. "Mom, Suzanne, Ryan, Marcus…?"

She pressed the phone to her ear. "Karen O'Connell. The office is now closed, so unless this is really—"

"Karen."

It was his voice. Deep, dark. It sucked her right back into that girl who had been nothing in his shadow. For a second, she had to remind herself to breathe. She somehow managed to turn her chair, because she couldn't let Owen see how rattled she was. No freaking out.

"Are you there?" he said.

She breathed out, having to remind herself that she hated this man, that he'd once called the cops on her because she wouldn't leave him be. His was a voice she'd never forget. Her heart was pounding. "Yes, I'm here. Why are you calling?"

Owen was listening, she knew.

"So you know who this is?" the man said.

Of course she did. What was it about the voice of Jack Curtis, the first man she'd ever loved, the one she'd married, who'd broken her heart?

"You know what?" she said. "This really isn't a good time for me, so if you don't mind…" She went to turn around and hang up.

"Wait, don't hang up. I need your help. And you know I wouldn't call you unless the situation were really…dire."

She didn't have to turn in her chair to know her brother was more than listening to everything she was saying—and everything she wasn't. She lowered her voice. "What I remember is that I'm not supposed to be talking to you. You made sure of that with the last set of cops. You've made your feelings for me very, very clear, so if you don't mind, I'm going to hang up now." She started to turn around again.

"Wait, Karen, don't hang up. Look, I'm sorry, but I'm in trouble—the kind of trouble that has me calling the last woman I would expect to help me."

"No, you look. I don't know what this is or what kind of trouble you're in, but let me remind you clearly of your words to me: You hate me, you want nothing to do with me, ever, and you never want to hear from me, talk to me, or see me again. In other words, I was and am very much dead to you, and—"

"I'm in jail," Jack said. "I've been charged with murder. I didn't do it."

She found herself staring at the phone for a second before putting it back to her ear.

"So if you could put everything aside, please," he said, "because I need your help."

She just lifted her gaze to the ceiling and leaned back in the chair, very aware of how her end of the conversation likely sounded to her brother.

"Hello, Karen, are you there?" he said. "Don't talk. Just listen. This is my one phone call. I'm in Sweetwater County Jail, and I'm stuck here until I go before a judge Monday morning. You know what that means."

"Why me?" She let out a sigh.

"Because there's something else you don't know," he started. She thought she heard someone in the background. "Look, I've got to go. Please, Karen, just please, show up."

The line went dead, and she pulled the phone from her ear before turning her chair around and setting the receiver back in the cradle. It took her another second to ground herself enough to look at her brother. His confusion was in his expression.

"You want to tell me what that was about?" Owen gestured to the phone and settled his feet back on the floor, not pulling his gaze from her. "Sounded to me like trouble. You in trouble? Something happened? Who aren't you supposed to contact? You know I can call Marcus…"

She found herself shaking her head. "It's someone I haven't heard from in years, something that ended badly. You know that one person you never want to hear from, and then they call? Well, he called because he just landed in a shitload of trouble."

Owen didn't seem convinced. "Sounded like more than that, Karen. You may as well just tell me, because I'll figure it out."

She took in her desk, the empty glass, and her brother, who didn't seem too interested in moving. "That was my husband," she said. "He's apparently in jail. I haven't talked to him in years. He hates me, and I hate him. He called the cops on me, got a restraining order. Things ended very, very badly, and I never expected to hear from him again, but hey…" She gestured to the phone as if that explained everything. She could honestly say she'd never seen Owen appear so shocked. He didn't wear it well.

"Right, good, glad to have this talk," she said. "So, since you're struggling to find something to say, let me help you. You're right to think I didn't tell anyone I got married. I hid it from all of you. At the time, it was a stupid-ass thing to do, a time in my life when I was doing stupid-ass things. Is there more to the story? Yes, absolutely. If you could just keep this little bombshell to yourself…"

Owen exhaled and looked around for a second as if trying to understand what she'd said. "I think you'd better start at the beginning," he replied. "And this time, Karen, don't leave anything out."

About the Author

"Lorhainne Eckhart is one of my go to authors when I want a guaranteed good book. So many twists and turns, but also so much love and such a strong sense of family."

(Lora W., Reviewer)

New York Times & USA Today bestseller Lorhainne Eckhart writes Raw Relatable Real Romance is best known for her big family romances series, where "Morals and family are running themes. Danger, romance, and a drive to do what is right will see you glued to the page." As one fan calls her, she is the "Queen of the family saga." (aherman) writing "the ups and downs of what goes on within a family but also with some suspense, angst and of course a bit of romance thrown in for good measure." Follow Lorhainne on Bookbub to receive alerts on New Releases and Sales and join her mailing list at LorhainneEckhart.com for her Monday Blog, books news, giveaways and FREE reads. With over 120 books, audiobooks, and multiple series published and available at all retailers now translated into six languages. She is a multiple recipient of the Readers' Favorite Award for Suspense and Romance, and lives in the Pacific Northwest on an island, is the mother of three, her oldest has autism and she is an advocate for never giving up on your dreams.

"Lorhainne Eckhart has this uncanny way of just hitting the spot every time with her books."

(Caroline L., Reviewer)

The O'Connells: *The O'Connells of Livingston, Montana are not your typical family. A riveting collection of stories surrounding the ups and downs of what goes on within a family but also with some suspense, angst and of course a bit of romance thrown in for good measure "I thought I loved the Friessens, but I absolutely adore the O'Connell's. Each and every book has totally different genres of stories but the one thing in common is how she is able to wrap it around the family which is the heart of each story." (C. Logue)*

The Friessens: *An emotional big family romance series, the Friessen family siblings find their relationships tested, lay their hearts on the line, and discover lasting love! "Lorhainne Eckhart is one of my go to authors when I want a guaranteed good book. So many twists and turns, but also so much love and such a strong sense of family." (Lora W., Reviewer)*

The Parker Sisters: *The Parker Sisters are a close-knit family, and like any other family they have their ups and downs. "Eckhart has crafted another intense family drama…The character development is outstanding, and the emotional investment is high…" (Aherman, Reviewer)*

The McCabe Brothers: *Join the five McCabe siblings on their journeys to the dark and dangerous side of love! An intense, exhilarating collection of romantic thrillers you won't want to miss. — "Eckhart has a new series that is definitely worth the read. The queen of the family saga started this series with a spin-off of her wildly successful Friessen series." From a Readers' Favorite award-winning author and "queen of the family saga" (Aherman)*

Lorhainne loves to hear from her readers! You can connect with me at:
www.LorhainneEckhart.com
lorhainneeckhart.le@gmail.com

CPSIA information can be obtained
at www.ICGtesting.com
Printed in the USA
BVHW041029030822
643617BV00025B/268